A MOMENT LIKE THIS

When Jenna Maitland's cousin Joss flees the responsibilities of their family's department store empire in Yorkshire, he escapes to Cornwall to follow his true calling and paint. Accompanied by the mysterious Gil Ryder, Jenna sets off south to find him. Once in Cornwall, Jenna finds herself becoming increasingly attracted to Gil — but is warned off by the attractive Victoria Symington, who appears to regard Gil as her own. Meanwhile, Joss's whereabouts has been discovered — but he is refusing to return . . .

RENA GEORGE

A
MOMENT
LIKE THIS

Complete and Unabridged

LINFORD
Leicester

First published in Great Britain in 2015

First Linford Edition
published 2016

A catalogue record for this book is available
from the British Library.

ISBN 978–1–4448–2908–2

1

Jenna Maitland was aware that he'd been watching her. If he hadn't been so good-looking she wouldn't have been bothered — but this man couldn't be ignored. She took in the immaculate dark suit, crisp white shirt and soft pink tie. Under his dark gaze, she could feel her cheeks begin to burn.

Determined not to embarrass herself, she forced her attention back to wrapping the expensive, limited-edition Lowry print her customer had just purchased. But in her peripheral vision she was still aware of him moving about the gallery. Suddenly, he turned and caught her looking at him. For a second, Jenna's professional response faltered, and she gave him a hesitant smile. The man's appraising brown eyes flickered over her, and his mouth twitched in the trace of a responding smile before he turned away to wander back up the gallery. Every now and then he'd stop to study one or other of the collection of Impressionist watercolours on display. Jenna suspected from his body language that he was simply marking time, waiting for her customer to leave before approaching her. It sent a deliciously icy tingle up her spine.

The customer had noticed him too, for more than once she had glanced back, her eyes lingering on the man's wide shoulders, the dark, well-groomed hair.

Over the years, Daniel Maitland's Kensington gallery had become popular with the trendy London set, and some of them even recognized the quality of the artwork they purchased — although Jenna still had to keep her frustration in check when paintings she adored were selected purely on the merit of their decorative ability to fit into the colour schemes of smart city apartments. But this man wasn't one of them; and neither, she suspected, was he an art collector. She was intrigued to discover exactly why he *was* here in her father's gallery. Her customer seemed in no hurry to leave. The new print would be perfect, she told Jenna, for that space on the wall behind the desk in her husband's study . . . or maybe above the hall table? She wavered, still unsure.

Jenna did her best to keep up, but the man's presence was disturbing. At last the customer picked up her package and turned to leave, throwing one final glance in the stranger's direction. He waited until the door swung closed again before turning and strolling towards Jenna. For a long moment they faced each other, neither of them speaking . . . then he smiled, and Jenna felt herself go weak at the knees.

She swallowed. 'Can I help you, sir?'

The compelling brown eyes were studying her and she felt her mouth go dry.

'I hope so.' His smile was slightly crooked, giving him a disarmingly rakish air, but his mouth was wide and sensitive. It was a nice mouth. 'I'm interested in purchasing something for a new apartment; perhaps you could offer some advice?'

Jenna inclined her head in a gesture inviting him to walk with her through the gallery. She didn't dare speak for fear her voice would come out in a squeak. What was wrong with her, for heaven's sake? It wasn't as if she was a stranger to the company of attractive men — even devastatingly handsome ones like this. His eyes were still openly appraising, taking in Jenna's smooth, dark hair, her elegantly-cut cream suit, and the expensive gold locket at her throat.

His voice was educated; its tone soft, but assertive; and there was the merest hint of an accent that Jenna couldn't place. She crossed the floor, indicating they should carry on up the gallery as she described the paintings on display and told him about the artists.

Then he pointed to a black-and-white geometric design by a young artist her father was nurturing. 'I'll have this one,' he said.

She smiled. 'Good choice. I'll have it wrapped. Shall we send it on to you?'

They'd moved back to the desk and Jenna flicked through the red leather ledger, getting ready to take his address, but he said nothing and she looked up. Under his amused gaze she was in danger of blushing like a schoolgirl. She cleared her throat and repeated, 'Do you want us to deliver the painting?'

'Can you send it here?' He put a business card on the large oak reception desk. Jenna picked it up, glancing briefly at the Covent Garden address before placing the card in the ledger.

He smiled, and laugh lines creased his mouth. The gorgeous eyes twinkled. He held out his hand. 'I'm Gil Ryder.' He nodded back to the sign above the gallery. 'I take it you're not Daniel Maitland.'

'I'm his daughter, Jenna,' she said, a little more stiffly than she had intended.

He smiled. 'I was just off for lunch,

Jenna. Perhaps you could be persuaded to join me?'

The invitation caught her off guard. 'I can't leave the gallery,' she stammered, annoyed by the audacity of this stranger, yet intrigued by his cheek.

But the man was not to be put off. He tilted his head, brown eyes glinting with mischief. 'Come on,' he said teasingly. 'Even the boss's daughter has to eat.' He arched an eyebrow. 'What do you say?'

She glanced at the clock. It *was* nearly lunchtime, and Claire, the gallery's assistant manager, would be coming on duty at any minute. If she let the man walk away now she might never see him again. Suddenly that seemed quite important. What was she waiting for? Of course she would let him take her to lunch. Ignoring the funny way her heart was flipping over, and avoiding his gaze, she shrugged and said, 'Why not?'

She'd expected they would walk to one of the excellent nearby restaurants, but Gil Ryder hailed a taxi and told the driver to take them to Covent Garden. She'd been to a couple of the bistros there, but the one he shepherded her into was new to her. It looked expensive. As they weaved their way through the tables, she could feel Gil's eyes on her back, and a tingle ran down her spine.

They both ordered steak with a crisp green salad, followed by a strawberry roulade. Jenna wasn't quite sure what to make of this man. She studied his handsome profile as he turned to summon the wine waiter. He had a strong face, a good, firm jawline — a man who knew what he wanted, and was probably used to getting it.

He turned back suddenly and caught her studying him again. His eyebrow lifted just a fraction and the hint of a smile twitched at the corners of his mouth. Jenna felt the blush start in her throat and travel up to her face with alarming speed. She was trying not to look flustered, but he reached across

7

and caught her hand.

'It's alright, you know. I can understand why you're suspicious of me.' He released her hand and sat back, watching her. 'Maybe I was a bit forward, inviting you for lunch when we'd only just met. And this place . . . ' He flipped a hand around the room. 'You're wondering why I brought you to a place like this.' She glanced around. 'Perhaps we should have come to somewhere a little less . . . ' The mesmerizing eyes narrowed as he searched for the right word. ' . . . a little less ostentatious, maybe.'

She was about to tell him she didn't actually object to their surroundings, when he cut in again.

'It's partly your fault, though, Jenna,' he said, waving his hand in a gesture to indicate her stylish appearance. 'Where else could I bring such a lady?'

Jenna's eyes examined his face. He was teasing her, but she didn't care. She giggled. 'I think you're making fun of me.'

'Hardly,' he said, quietly.

Jenna felt the flush creep up her neck again.

The waiter arrived with the wine, and after Gil had tasted a sample and nodded his approval, Jenna's glass was filled.

They ate in virtual silence, savouring the delicious food. The coffee Gil later ordered arrived rich and fragrant, and came with mint-flavoured chocolates.

Jenna stirred her cup, glancing up at him. 'That was absolutely wonderful. I feel thoroughly spoiled now.'

He leaned forward, smiling. 'Spoiled enough to want to do it again?' His look was teasing but she knew he was being serious.

She wasn't about to refuse, but to her surprise he lifted a hand to stop her speaking. 'There's something you should know before you answer that.' He put a hand across his heart and smiled. 'I'm actually here as . . . well, as a kind of knight errant, I suppose.'

Jenna stared at him. 'I don't understand.'

'I'm here because your Aunt Molly asked me to come.'

Jenna's mouth fell open. 'You know Molly?'

He nodded. 'The plan was to persuade your father to go to Cornwall and find your cousin, Joss.'

Jenna's hands went up in a gesture of confusion. 'Wait a minute. I haven't a clue what you're talking about. What's all this about Joss? Can you start at the beginning?'

'I'm sorry. I thought you knew about all this.'

'All what?' She could feel her impatience rising.

Gil glanced around the restaurant. A few of the other diners were casting curious glances in their direction. 'Look,' he said, 'we need to take this somewhere more private.' He signalled for the bill. 'I know someone just round the corner who'd love to meet you.'

Jenna said nothing for a moment, trying to work out what was going on. She'd thought he'd been attracted to *her*, wanted *her* company over lunch. It was all now looking like something completely different. Some Maitland family drama seemed to be unfolding all around her, and she wasn't sure she was going to like what this stranger had to tell her.

She gave him an icy stare. 'I think you've got some explaining to do, Mr Ryder.'

'You're right, it's time I came clean.' He put his hands up in a gesture of defence. 'But please don't judge me until you hear the whole story.'

Jenna reached for her bag and stood up with him.

When they were outside, he took her hand. 'Come on,' he said, leading her across the cobbled piazza. 'There's someone I want you to meet.'

They'd walked less than fifty yards when he stopped in front of an artisan craft shop, its window displaying an array of beautiful hand-made pottery. Jenna noticed the shop name — 'Ryder's'.

A bell tinkled as they went in, and an

attractive woman with shining chestnut hair and smiling brown eyes hurried forward to greet them. 'This is Caroline,' Gil said.

Jenna's mind flashed back to the 'Ryder' name above the shop, and struggled to fight down rising disappointment. The woman was older than Gil . . . but certainly not enough to be his mother. Was this his wife? She put out her hand and forced a smile. 'I'm pleased to meet you, Mrs Ryder.'

'Ms Ryder,' Caroline corrected. 'I'm Gil's sister.'

Jenna knew Gil was watching her, and she glanced around the shop to cover her embarrassment. 'You have some lovely things here.'

'Thank you. We're lucky enough to be trusted with the work of some of the best craftsmen and -women in the country.'

'Caroline knows Joss,' Gil cut in. 'That's why I wanted you to meet her.'

Jenna raised her eyebrow.

Caroline smiled. 'Thanks to Gil's

constant invitations to Yorkshire, I've spent quite a bit of time with Molly and Isaac . . . and Joss and Francine, of course.'

'You've stayed at Fenfleet?' Jenna's voice rose in surprise.

Caroline nodded, calling into the back of the shop for her assistant to take over. She led the way into a back room, and turned to fill a coffee percolator.

Gil said, 'I should explain. I know the Maitlands rather well. In fact, I'm a director in the company. That's why I've come down to London. Molly and Isaac are desperate to know Joss is alright, so I've . . . '

Jenna threw up her hands. 'Wait a minute! Are you saying Joss is missing?'

Gil tried to hide a worried grimace. 'Not missing, exactly . . . more like AWOL.'

Jenna was horrified. 'What do you mean, AWOL? What about Francine . . . and the twins?' She watched as Gil's eyes clouded and he heaved a deep sigh.

'Well, they're not happy about the situation . . . obviously. But we're all trying to support them while we get this thing sorted out.'

Jenna pressed her fingers to her temples, trying to make sense of what she'd just heard. This was her family Gil was talking about!

She'd been ten when her mother died and her heartbroken father, not able to bear the grief, had taken off on a painting odyssey across Cornwall, leaving her to be brought up by Molly and Isaac. She could still hear the angry voices from the day he left.

'Your child needs you, Daniel! You can't abandon her like this!' It was her Aunt Molly.

Her Uncle Isaac's tone was bitter. 'If you leave now, then you're no brother of mine!'

None of them knew Jenna had been in the garden, tears rolling down her cheeks as she heard every word.

'I'm doing this for my daughter,' Daniel insisted, his voice cracking with

14

emotion. 'What good am I to her now? I can't look after a child. Jenna will be far happier with you here at Fenfleet.'

She'd tried to be brave that last day when her father took her in his arms. She knew he was crying as he walked away.

Suddenly aware that Gil and Caroline were both watching her, she swallowed. But Daniel had been right; she eventually did recover. And, though she never stopped missing him, she grew to accept that her father would not take her with him at the end of his regular visits.

Molly and Isaac had brought her up as though she was their own daughter. And as for Joss — well, he'd been more like a protective older brother than a cousin. She'd been Maid of Honour when he'd married Francine.

Jenna's hand flew to her mouth. Francine! All this would devastate her. She turned to Caroline. 'So when did you last see Joss?'

Caroline thought back. 'It was a few days before he went off. Francine had gone shopping in Leeds, and he took me to see the Harrogate store.' She cleared her throat and looked away, and Jenna wondered what Francine would have had to say about that.

'Joss loved hearing about other people's businesses,' Caroline added. 'He was forever encouraging me to talk about the Ryder shops.'

'There's more than one?' Jenna was surprised.

'We have two here in London,' Gil cut in.

Caroline threw her brother a good-natured grimace. 'When my brother says *we*, he means *me*. He's forgetting that I bought him out eighteen months ago so he could buy into the Maitlands' business.'

Gil nodded. 'Molly and Isaac took me on as a director because of my previous experience working in the City for one of the big merchant banks.' He smiled. 'My financial background comes in handy when you have three department stores to run.'

Jenna's eyes widened. 'You run the Maitland stores now? I thought Uncle Isaac and Aunt Molly and Joss did that?'

She thought she detected a flash of annoyance in the dark eyes. 'Of course they do. I was speaking figuratively. It's obviously still the Maitlands' business.'

'Did Joss tell you he was planning to leave?'

'Not a word,' Gil said. 'It was as much a shock to me as anyone. I thought he was happy that his parents trusted him with so much responsibility. I'd go as far as saying he just loved being immersed in the business.'

Jenna nodded. Yes, that was the Joss she knew. She frowned.

'I can't believe he'd just take off like this. Why would he do that to his family? He adores Francine and the children.'

Caroline placed two steaming mugs of coffee on the table, and pulled out one of the high stools from under a bench to perch opposite them.

Gil cleared his throat. 'He hasn't exactly disappeared without trace. Joss is in Cornwall . . . painting.'

Jenna stared at him. 'Painting!' Once again, visions of her father leaving her at Fenfleet that night flashed into her mind. Was it all happening again? Her brow furrowed. 'You said something about trying to persuade my father to find Joss?'

'That's right. Molly rang him. She said Joss has always looked up to Daniel . . . wanted to be like him.'

'An itinerant artist, you mean,' Jenna said with a wry grin. But Molly was right. When Joss was younger, he'd hero-worshipped his uncle Daniel — tried to emulate his painting skills, his rakish lifestyle . . . the twinkle in his eye that set so many female hearts fluttering.

She could see why Molly and Isaac wanted Daniel to go looking for Joss. He was the one her cousin was most likely to heed. 'My father should be on his way home today from an exhibition in Paris. I'm sure he'll do all he can to help when I explain things.'

Gil cleared his throat. 'The thing is . . . ' He hesitated. 'Molly has already asked him, and . . . '

'Don't tell me he refused?' Jenna's eyes were blazing.

Gil nodded.

Jenna puffed out her cheeks. What was Daniel thinking? He couldn't refuse to go to Cornwall. She wouldn't let him refuse.

'Leave Daniel to me,' she said.

Gil held her gaze, his eyes smiling. 'Thanks, Jenna. I was hoping that's what you would say.' The sound of her name on his lips sent a warm glow racing through her body.

As they walked through to the front of the shop, the door tinkled and two more customers came in.

Gil bent to kiss his sister's cheek. 'We can see you're busy. I'll call you,' he said as they went out.

'Your sister's nice. I like her.'

'Yes, I thought you might. That's why I wanted you two to meet.'

'What I don't understand is, why all the subterfuge at the gallery? Why all the pretence about wanting to buy a painting?'

'But I do want that painting. It's for Caroline's new apartment.'

He waved down a taxi and they got in, exchanged mobile numbers, and promised to keep in touch. Jenna wondered if he'd kiss her when they parted, but he didn't. As she stood on the pavement outside the gallery watching the black cab pull back into the traffic, he rolled down the window and called back, 'Good luck with your dad.'

2

Daniel Maitland made no concessions to his fifty-seven years. His dark, but greying, hair was still long, caught at the nape of his neck by a rubber band. His linen jacket, over a loose, collarless grey shirt, was crumpled from his journey. A red spotted kerchief was knotted at his throat, and the battered Panama hat he insisted on wearing sat at a jaunty angle. He threw his arms wide to Jenna as he came into the gallery.

'You didn't manage to burn the place down, then?' He grinned, looking round.

Jenna gave an exasperated sigh. 'I want to talk to you,' she said, grabbing his hand and calling back to Claire to look after the gallery as she dragged her father into the back room.

Daniel screwed up his eyes. 'OK.

What have I done now?'

'What's all this about you refusing to help Molly and Isaac find Joss?' she demanded.

Daniel grimaced. 'Ah . . . it's about that, then.' He shrugged. 'Joss is a grown man. If he wants to take himself off to Cornwall, then it's his business.'

'That's a bit harsh,' Jenna said. 'What about Francine and the twins? Don't you think we should try to help them?'

'My darling girl, do you really think that I would refuse to help if I thought I could do any good? This is none of my business.' He shrugged. 'Joss is a free spirit. If he wants to take off to Cornwall to paint, then who am I to say he shouldn't?'

Jenna sighed. 'So you're saying there's nothing you can do?' She was trying not to be shocked.

Daniel sat back down in his chair. 'I didn't say that.' He smiled and Jenna saw the twinkle in his eyes. 'I could send you to Cornwall in my place.'

Her eyes widened. 'Me?'

'Why not? You and Joss always got on — and I imagine Francine would welcome a shoulder to cry on. I think you should go to Yorkshire first, though. Spend some time with the family and get the real story before you go rushing off to Cornwall.'

'Francine might think I'm interfering.'

Daniel got up and crossed the room to the little wooden table where he kept a drinks tray. He poured himself a substantial whisky and came back to sit opposite his daughter. 'We both know she won't think that. Besides, I'm sure Molly and Isaac would much rather see you than look at my ugly face.'

'But what about the gallery?'

'Claire can manage. She's quite capable, you know.' He lifted the glass and drank back a finger of whisky before thumping it back on the table with a satisfied sigh. 'And I'll be so busy in my studio, I'll hardly even notice you've gone.'

Jenna chewed her bottom lip as she considered the idea. It was true. She'd get a warm welcome . . . and she could talk to Francine, offer her help. If it was declined, then she would at least have done something. 'OK,' she declared. 'I'll drive up there first thing tomorrow.'

'Just one thing, though, Jenna,' Daniel Maitland warned. 'I don't want you to feel bad if you can't persuade Joss to go home. It won't be your fault, so just you take care.'

'Of course I will,' she said, throwing a questioning glance at her father. 'Are you sure you'll manage on your own?'

Daniel's eyebrow lifted in a warning glare. 'OK,' she laughed, 'I get the message. You'll be fine.' She slid her arms around his neck and gave him a peck on the cheek before turning to run upstairs to pack.

The gallery had been a second-hand shop when Daniel bought the premises four years earlier, and even though he'd wanted Jenna to join him, he hadn't suggested it because she was now so happy with her Yorkshire family. The Maitland stores were prospering, and Isaac was grooming Jenna to play a leading role in the company. She'd been put in charge of the York store, where her innovative ideas were putting it ahead of its rivals.

Daniel poured himself another whisky and brooded. It had been selfish of him to accept her offer of help when the gallery ran into trouble two years ago. But she had insisted on leaving Yorkshire and moving in with him. A wry smile crossed his still-handsome, craggy face. His daughter was stubborn, but with her steadying hand at the helm, the gallery had come slowly back to life and was now an acknowledged success.

He could hear the movement upstairs as she packed. He knew Molly and Isaac had really wanted to ask Jenna for help. Contacting him had been their way of keeping him involved, but they knew he was always going to stand aside in favour of his daughter.

Jenna's excitement grew as she folded

things into her case. She was going back to Fenfleet. It would be good to see the family again, even if she wished the circumstances were different. What was Joss up to? Memories of idyllic days when the pair of them cycled through the leafy lanes around the family's big old country house drifted back. Sometimes Francine had joined them on those outings . . . a pretty, bubbly, blonde girl that Joss was spending more and more time with. Jenna thought they made the perfect couple.

She set off early next morning to avoid the worst of the London traffic, and her spirits soared as she headed north. They'd been so busy at the gallery that she hadn't managed to get back to Yorkshire for the past six months. It felt like a lifetime ago now. But this time her eagerness to see the family again was tinged with foreboding. What would she say to Francine?

She reached York by mid-morning, and less than an hour later was driving between the high stone pillars that marked the entrance to Fenfleet. The house came into view as she rounded the bend in the drive. It never failed to take her breath away. She took in the two symmetrical gables, each with five traditional wooden sash windows, the smallest ones being on their own under the eaves. The stonework was weathered because the house had stood on this spot for centuries.

Molly was on the front steps, and before Jenna's little white Fiesta had even stopped, she was hurrying forward to greet her. 'Daniel rang and told us you were coming.' She held Jenna at arms' length as she gave her an appraising look. 'My, you look so well. I can't tell you how pleased Isaac and I are to have you back again, darling.'

'How is Isaac?' Jenna asked, as the two women linked arms and went into the house.

'Very angry. What Joss has done is outrageous. We can't imagine what he's thinking, going off like this. Poor Francine is in bits. She's been holding off telling the children. They think their father is away on business.'

'Is Francine here?'

Molly shook her head. 'She's gone into town. I suggested she should. It might help take her mind off things for an hour or two.'

Jenna doubted it would do that, but she could imagine Molly insisting, and smiled.

Despite the size of Fenfleet, the house always managed to have a cosy feel. There was something intimate and vital about it. A vase of lilac-coloured stock sat on a polished table, filling the high-ceilinged hall with fragrance. The double doors of the drawing room were open, and she could see through to the French windows and glimpses of yellow roses scrambling over the garden balustrade. She wanted to run out and bury her face in their scent.

'There's a call for you, Molly,' a familiar male voice behind her said. 'I can help Jenna with her things.'

Jenna spun round and caught her

breath. 'Gil! I didn't expect to find you here.' She'd been so preoccupied with thoughts of Joss, and how upset Francine and the rest of them would be at his sudden departure, that she'd forgotten Gil was also now part of the Maitland business.

'I have a cottage just down the road,' he explained. 'Not quite as grand as this, of course, but it suits me.' He nodded towards the still-open front door. 'If you give me your car keys, I'll fetch your case. They tell me you're in your old room on the first floor. I'll see you up there.'

Her shoes sank into the red carpet as she moved along the oak-panelled corridor, passing doors on either side, and stopped at what had been her old room. She pushed the door open and light flooded the dark passage. Seconds later Gil appeared, carrying her two cream leather cases. He put them down and came towards her.

'It's good to see you again, Jenna.' She noticed the catch in his voice and looked up. He was standing very close, and Jenna could feel her heart pounding. He reached out and, using a finger, gently moved aside a stray tendril of dark hair from her face.

'I'm glad you've come,' he said, quietly.

Jenna looked away, hoping he hadn't noticed that her cheeks were burning.

'I don't suppose anyone's heard any more from Joss?' Her voice sounded strange.

'No, nothing's changed.' He sighed. 'Except, of course, that Francine is getting more stressed out by the day.'

'Does she know I'm here?'

'Yes, Molly told her. Isaac is still at the York store, but I think he'll be back early tonight. I know he wants to see you.' He stepped back. 'I expect you'll want to rest after your long drive.'

'I can do that later, but I would like to tidy up before going back downstairs.'

Gil nodded. 'Take your time,' he called as he headed for the door. 'Come down when you're ready.'

When the door closed behind him, Jenna wandered about the huge room. It had been redecorated since she last slept here. The walls were now a pastel green and there was a new cream carpet, giving the room a restful feel. The dressing table and bedside chests of antique oak, as was the huge wardrobe, hadn't changed. Jenna thought of her tiny bedroom above the London gallery and smiled. She wondered what her father was doing now.

From the window, she could see across the formal front garden and wondered who kept it in such immaculate condition these days. Fenfleet was as beautiful as ever. Jenna still expected to hear a gong resound through the house at any moment, announcing that luncheon was served. But it was Gil who did that, with a quiet knock on her door.

'The family usually have a drink before eating.'

'I know.' She grinned. 'I used to live

here . . . remember?'

Gil pulled a contrite face and scowled. 'I stand corrected . . . but we'll still be having drinks downstairs when you care to join us.'

Jenna watched him leave, and sat on the edge of the bed until the fluttering performance her wayward heart seemed to go through every time she saw him began to subside. She reminded herself that she was here for Francine and Joss. However difficult it might be, her own feelings would have to be set aside for now.

She felt grubby after her drive, so had a quick wash in the pristine white en suite bathroom, then ran a brush through her hair before joining the others in the drawing room. Molly was sipping a glass of sherry as she sat on one of the two large cream leather sofas that faced each other on either side of the ornate marble fireplace. Jenna had a sudden memory of a Christmas morning twelve years before when she had stared at gaily-wrapped presents beneath a glittering tree. It was the first Christmas after her mother died, and she'd never felt so alone in her life. But Molly had known instinctively what she was feeling, and had come to slip an arm round Jenna's shoulder as she drew her into the family group. Her father had made a surprise appearance that Christmas and presented her with a set of paints in a smart wooden box. Isaac had scowled, but Joss said it was the best present he had ever seen and wished it had been given to him. The tubes of paint were squeezed dry now, and the box was covered in a messy stain of colours. But it was still on the top shelf of her wardrobe at home.

Gil was dispensing drinks from a small table. Francine had returned from her shopping trip and was by the French windows. Jenna was shocked to see how pale and drawn she looked, but her pretty face lit up when she saw her husband's cousin. She came forward to give a welcoming hug. She felt so thin and frail.

Gil approached with two glasses of

sherry and handed one to each of them.

'There's no point in beating about the bush,' Molly said from the sofa. 'This business with Joss has shaken us all.'

Jenna saw Francine's bottom lip tremble as she laid her glass very carefully on the table. 'I'm not feeling very hungry, Molly. Do you mind if I skip lunch?'

She touched Jenna's arm as she went through the French doors into the garden. Jenna knew she'd be heading for the bungalow in the grounds that had been Isaac and Molly's wedding present to her and Joss.

'I'll just make sure she's alright,' Jenna said, hurrying after Francine.

She found her in her kitchen, sitting forlornly at a big scrubbed pine table. She glanced up and gave her a crooked smile. 'Molly told me you were coming. I thought Daniel might be, too.'

'Just me.' She grinned back. 'And I'm here to help, so just tell me what I can do.'

Francine shrugged. She'd put the kettle on and it was now boiling, but she showed no interest in doing anything with it.

'Tea,' Jenna said decisively, striding towards the kettle. 'That's what we need here.' She busied herself finding cups, playing for time before mentioning Joss. She didn't want to get this wrong.

'I appreciate you coming, Jenna, but there's nothing you can do,' Francine said as Jenna placed the mug of tea in front of her. 'Joss has left us and there's nothing anybody can do about it.'

Jenna sat opposite, staring at the sad, wan face. 'That's defeatist talk, Francine. There's always something that can be done. Has anyone actually gone to talk to Joss? I assume you all know where he is? Gil said something about him going to Cornwall to paint.'

Francine nodded. 'That's what he's told everybody. He was always taking off into the moors with his sketchbook.'

Jenna smiled. 'I remember,' she said,

as a vision came to mind of the cycling expeditions the three of them used to make, puffing up the hilly winding country roads with Joss's sketchbook poking out from his saddlebag.

'It was a good cover story,' Francine said, with a heavy sigh. 'Joss wants everybody to believe he's following his dream to paint. But I know different.'

Jenna frowned. 'I don't understand.'

Francine was staring, unseeing, at a spot on the other side of the room. 'Joss and I have had a bit of a rocky time lately,' she began. 'Isaac's health hasn't been good these past months, and he's been taking a back seat in the running of the business, which has meant more and more responsibility being pushed onto Joss's shoulders. He's been working long hours, coming home exhausted and snapping at everybody.'

She sighed and pushed her fingers through her curly blonde hair. 'I was worried he was heading for a breakdown.'

'But didn't the rest of the family

notice how much stress he was under?'

Francine shrugged. 'You know Joss. He's always been good at hiding his feelings. The last thing he wanted was to give Molly and Isaac any idea that he couldn't cope.'

Jenna thought of Gil. She was sure that nothing much would get past those shrewd, dark eyes. So why hadn't he stepped in to help? Maybe Joss had just taken off to give himself the space to sort his head out.

'Well at least you know where he is. It's not as if he's disappeared or anything.'

'Oh, he's been in touch. The day after he left, he rang to say he was in St Ives and trying to find a place to rent. He said he was planning to spend his time painting.' Francine's bottom lip quivered and tears trembled in her blue eyes. 'Oh, Jenna. I don't think he's coming back.'

'Well, of course he is,' Jenna said, reaching across the table to touch her friend's hand.

But Francine pulled it back. 'You don't understand,' she sniffed. 'Joss is not alone in Cornwall! He's . . . he's with a woman!'

She raised a hand to fend off Jenna's disbelieving protest. 'It's true,' she said, flatly. 'They've been seen together.'

'Who's seen them?' Jenna demanded.

'One of Joss's cricketing pals, a man called Guy Bradford. He turned up one day on the pretext of wanting to see Joss, but I could tell he was lying. I've never liked the man — too flash, too well-off, too full of himself.' She grimaced. 'I'm sure you know the type.'

Jenna nodded. 'Thinks he's God's gift?'

'Exactly,' said Francine. 'I could see he was just dying to tell me something. He said he was being a friend, and that I should know about Joss's other woman. He'd seen them together in Joss's old Jeep. It was the day he left.'

'But that could have been anything. Joss could have been giving someone a lift.'

But Francine's head was shaking. 'Guy saw them kissing.'

'Maybe he was lying.'

'No, he was enjoying the moment too much. He'd seen them together alright.'

'And you think Joss is with this other woman in Cornwall?'

Francine spread her hands in a gesture of helplessness. 'I'm trying desperately not to believe it, but . . . Oh, Jenna, I just don't know what to think.'

'Maybe you should go down there and confront him?'

'I haven't got the courage.' She looked up, her eyes pleading. 'But you have. Will you go to Cornwall and find Joss for me, Jenna? Will you do that?'

Jenna stood up. If she'd been unsure before about how she could help, she was in no doubt now. She would leave for St Ives in the morning.

As she turned to go, Francine caught her arm. 'You won't mention this other woman to the family, will you? They'll have to know eventually, of course, but just not yet.'

There was panic in her voice, and Jenna smiled reassuringly. 'I won't say a word. And I will go to see Joss — if that's what you want?'

Francine nodded and gave her a hug. 'I'm so glad you've come,' she said.

Molly and Gil had finished lunch by the time Jenna got back to them. Gil stood up as she came into the room. 'How is she?'

'Worried. She's asked me to go down to Cornwall to see Joss. I'll be leaving first thing in the morning.'

Molly's hand fluttered at her throat. 'Well, thank heavens for that. Isaac and I were hoping you would do this.' She got up and gathered Jenna into her arms. 'Bring our boy home,' she whispered, her voice choked.

Jenna glanced across the room to where Gil was watching them. She imagined she caught a flash of annoyance in the brown eyes. But then he smiled, and her heart began to thud. 'I'll drive you there,' he said.

Both women stared at him. 'You want

to come with me to Cornwall?' Jenna could hear the shake in her voice.

'If that's alright with you. We needn't stay together down there. Just think of me as a taxi.'

'What a great idea.' Molly beamed at them.

Jenna's heart was thudding even louder now. 'Well . . . if you're sure . . . '

3

Neither of them spoke much on the long drive south, but — although Jenna caught Gil glancing in her direction a couple of times — the silence between them was comfortable. He seemed to sense her need for quiet, for time to think. Francine's story had disturbed her. The man she'd heard described wasn't the Joss she'd grown up with: the Joss who had taught her to climb trees, track foxes and recognize the calls of all the wild birds around Fenfleet. That Joss was kind, gentle and easy-going — the last man she believed capable of cheating on his wife. There just had to be another explanation. She tried to picture Joss's face when she turned up at his door. She'd been told he didn't want his family tracking him down. Did that include her? Would he be angry when he saw her? And how would she feel if she walked into some kind of cosy little love nest that Joss was sharing with another woman? She shivered.

Gil threw her a concerned glance. 'There's a blanket in the back, if you're cold,' he offered.

Jenna had been so deep in her own thoughts that his voice made her start. 'I'm fine, really. But thanks.' She glanced up at his handsome profile and a shiver of another kind tingled through her. The next few days could be difficult enough without the added complication of her growing feelings for the man beside her. For the first time since Gil's offer to drive her to Cornwall, she began to wonder what would happen when they actually arrived at their destination. He'd told her to think of him as no more than a taxi . . . but it was already too late for that. What if he booked them into the same hotel? A little tremor of excitement crept up her spine, and she tried to ignore it. She was here to help Joss and Francine!

The motorway sped past as Jenna

closed her eyes, enjoying the luxurious comfort of Gil's low-slung sports car. It was a lot more elegant than her Fiesta. But cars like this were part of his world — and they suited him.

He sensed she was relaxing, and smiled. 'I take it this won't be your first visit to Cornwall, Jenna?'

'Hardly,' she said. 'We used to come down here all the time when Mum was alive. We stayed in a little fishing village called Polperro . . . in a tiny white-washed cottage overlooking the harbour . . . ' Her voice trailed off as the memories of the happy, sun-splashed days rushed back.

'Sounds nice.'

Jenna sighed. 'It was idyllic, but then I suppose all happy family holidays seem like that when you're little.'

'And I imagine the memories are all the more precious when you lose one of your parents,' he said, in a voice so gentle that Jenna looked up at him. She could see the lump in his throat and wondered if he had also lost someone close.

'I was ten when my mum died,' she began, softly. 'Dad couldn't cope with bringing up a young girl on his own, so he took me to Fenfleet, to Molly and Isaac. They brought me up like I was their own daughter. So Joss and I grew up together. He's like the elder brother I never had.'

Gil grinned down at her. 'You Maitlands are a close lot, aren't you?'

Jenna laughed. 'You don't want to get on the wrong side of us, that's for sure . . . not if you don't want the whole clan coming down on you.'

'Is that what your father did — get on the wrong side of the rest of the Maitlands?'

Jenna stared at him. 'He went his own way, if that's what you mean. Not everybody is cut out to run a business empire.' Her tone was sharp, and she was aware she was defending her father more fiercely than was necessary. She took a pause. 'The family owned two department stores at that time: one in York, the other in Harrogate. Both were much smaller than they are now. My grandfather left equal shares to Daniel and Isaac, but Dad was only interested in painting, so it was Isaac and Molly who built up the business and added that third Leeds store. Dad has only ever been a sleeping partner.'

Gil kept his eyes on the road. 'Do you think Joss is following in Daniel's footsteps? I mean, relinquishing the business to pursue a totally different lifestyle?'

Jenna frowned and bit her lip. 'I really don't know,' she said. But she had spent a lot of time wondering just that.

It was mid-morning when they reached the M5. Bypassing Bristol, they headed south to join the A30, which went all the way to Penzance. Soon they were driving through the bleak and beautiful Bodmin Moor.

'There's an old coaching inn up ahead where we can stop for some lunch,' Gil said.

Jenna nodded her consent. The thought of a snack, a drink, and somewhere to stretch her legs was suddenly irresistible.

The pub was on a hill overlooking a wide expanse of moorland. As Gil pulled into the car park, Jenna pointed to a lark soaring high above the wild heather moor. They stopped to watch it, leaning on a low stone wall and shielding their eyes from the sun until the bird disappeared from view. Then they turned to cross the cobbled courtyard, passing beneath a sign that told them they were entering the Smugglers' Bar.

Inside, it was dark and cosy, with low-beamed ceilings. A basket of logs stood by a vast inglenook fireplace, ready to kindle a blaze if the evenings grew chilly. The stone walls displayed tourist-friendly images of eighteenth-century smugglers leading over-burdened donkeys across the moors by moonlight. Jenny found a corner table while Gil went to the bar and ordered roast beef sandwiches, a coffee for Jenna, and a half-pint of lager for himself. As he waited, he glanced round and smiled at her. Embarrassed at having once again been caught watching him, Jenna felt her cheeks colour. She made an effort to recover her composure by the time he returned with their drinks.

'I love these old places,' Jenna said, glancing round the bar.

'Yes, it's great,' Gil agreed. 'But I didn't bring you here to talk about the pub.' He repositioned his glass on his beer mat before looking up at her. 'How did you think Isaac was looking?'

The question took her by surprise. It would have been a reflex action to answer 'Fine' — but, now that she thought about it, she wondered . . . His welcome to her, when he eventually arrived home from the York store last evening, had been as warm as ever. His face had creased into the familiar grin, but the normally-sharp blue eyes had looked tired. And she remembered that he'd felt thinner when she hugged him.

'He's been doing far too much, Jenna. Molly and I are quite worried about him.'

Jenna's brow wrinkled. According to Francine, Joss had left two weeks ago. His absence was bound to put more pressure on his father. She suddenly felt angry. How selfish of Joss not to have considered that. But she'd been as much to blame as anyone. She could have gone up to Yorkshire more often. Maybe if she had, she would also have noticed that Isaac was no longer as robust as he used to be.

Even now, she had been so focused on Joss and Francine's problems that she hadn't considered what his absence was doing to Molly and Isaac. She met Gil's eyes. 'Is Isaac really ill?' she asked quietly.

'Not ill, exactly, but he's not getting any younger and he needs to slow down. Molly has been trying to persuade him to take a back seat in the business.' He lifted his lager and Jenna watched the level go down in his glass as he swallowed. He put it down again. 'I was brought into the company to take some of the workload off Isaac and Joss.'

Jenna shrugged. 'So what's the problem?'

'The problem,' he sighed, 'is that there is only so much I can do. Joss needs to shoulder a lot more responsibility. You've no idea how many problems his absence has caused. Oh, I can handle the extra administrative stuff, the meetings and the store visits.' He grimaced. 'But I'm not a Maitland. And with Joss gone, Isaac is visualizing the family business, that he and Molly have devoted their lives to building up, crumbling before his eyes.'

'Poor Isaac. I should have noticed how much stress he was under.'

'You couldn't be expected to know any of this,' Gil said quietly. Their eyes met and he smiled. 'But now that you're here . . . '

'Well, I can't see what more I can do,' she said defensively.

He leant forward, his dark eyes searching hers. 'You're a Maitland, aren't you?'

She was — and she would have given

anything to be back in Yorkshire working alongside Isaac and Joss, helping to run the stores. The Maitlands' entrepreneurial spirit ran in her veins . . . but her father had needed her in London. And he had always come first with Jenna.

'I'm not part of the Maitlands' empire anymore,' she said stiffly.

Gil sighed. 'You're right. I'm sorry. I spoke out of turn.'

But his words were still chasing around her head as they drove through Cornwall. Her father was a Maitland too, and although Jenna knew he still held shares in the company, he wanted no responsibility in the running of it. But she'd made her decision. She ran a London gallery now, and, short of abandoning her father, she could see no way of helping Isaac — apart, that was, from persuading Joss to return home and shoulder his responsibilities.

It was mid-afternoon when they arrived in St Ives. Gil nodded up towards a couple of big hotels on the hill overlooking the bay. 'I can book you into one of those, if you like.'

Jenna turned to look at him. It was as though he had read her earlier thoughts. She said, 'What about you? Where are you going to stay?'

'Didn't I mention? I've already got accommodation down here. It's just you we have to get fixed up.'

It would have been reasonable to ask what accommodation he already had, but she didn't. Instead, she pointed ahead towards the old town and the harbour. 'I think I'd rather be more central. Can we try down here?'

It was August, and the narrow streets were teeming with tourists. No one bothered about staying on the pavements: these folk were on holiday, and the usual rules that roads were for cars and pavements for pedestrians didn't seem to apply. Negotiating the twisting, cramped streets, and expertly avoiding colliding with the masses, Gil's driving skills eventually got them onto the seafront. Jenna indicated a parking sign and they headed for it. An arrow directed them into a short-stay car park where they left Gil's car and joined the strolling crowds wandering along the shopping lane that ran parallel to the seafront. Paintings and framed prints of white sands and turquoise seas were everywhere.

Neither of them noticed the young blonde woman step into the shadow of a doorway as they approached, or felt the coldness of her green-eyed stare follow them to the end of the lane. They laughed as they turned down to the waterfront, and stopped by the railings to watch a group of aggressive seagulls squabbling over the remains of someone's discarded chip bag. Across the curve of the bay, Jenna could see the harbour wall stretching out into the sea. She took a deep breath. It was all so beautiful — and easy to understand why artists came to this place.

On their way back to the car, she noticed a pub down by the harbour. 'Let's have a drink,' she suggested.

Gil squinted at the place and nodded. 'Why not?' he agreed, following her into the pub's dark interior. The place was so crowded that they had to wait for a table. The glass of chilled wine he brought back to her tasted delicious, and a mellow glow was beginning to filter around her insides. She sat up, her face animated as the idea suddenly struck her. 'I'd like to stay here. Do you think they might have a room?'

Gil's brow wrinkled as he glanced round the crowded bar. 'Are you sure? It's not exactly quiet.'

But Jenna was remembering the clink of the boats just outside the door. It was just the kind of area Joss would choose to live in. 'I'm sure,' she said. 'This is the place.'

She went with Gil to the bar and waited as he asked the barman if they had guest accommodation. He nodded, moving to the end of the counter to retrieve a large black diary before flicking through the pages until he found the one he was looking for.

'No singles available, I'm afraid, but we do have a nice double with a view across the harbour.'

Jenna smiled. 'Sounds perfect.' She rummaged in her bag for a pen to fill in her registration details. 'I'm not sure how long I'll be staying. Can we leave it open-ended?'

'No problem,' the barman said. 'And the name's Mike, by the way.'

'I'm Jenna,' she said, offering her hand. She knew Gil was frowning as he watched her. Since he'd already organized his own accommodation, she was now free to go her own way, and she intended to do just that. Gil's offer to drive her down to Cornwall had obviously been just that, since he had no intention of staying with her.

She turned to him and forced her most brilliant smile. 'I'll be fine now,' she said. 'If you could just fetch my case in . . . '

When he returned, carrying Jenna's smart leather case, he paused to take another look around the bar. 'I'm not sure I like leaving you here on your own, Jenna.'

'Oh, for heaven's sake,' she tutted. 'I'm a big girl. And, as you so rightly reminded me earlier, Gil . . . I'm a Maitland. And I can cope just fine.'

She saw his eyebrow arch, and imagined she'd caught a glint of amusement in his mesmerizing dark eyes. 'Yes,' he said slowly, 'I can see that. Anyway, you have my number. Call me any time . . . day or night.'

His muscular frame filled the door space, and as she watched him duck below the low lintel, she had a sudden feeling of loneliness.

'Your boyfriend not staying, then?' the barman said.

Jenna was still staring after Gil. 'Not this time,' she said.

She turned to head up to her room, and then paused, looking back. 'I don't suppose you know a Joss Maitland . . . ? He's an artist.'

'So is half the population of St Ives,'

Mike grinned, stacking clean glasses on the shelves behind the bar.

She gave a shrug. She hadn't really expected to strike lucky with her first enquiry. If Joss was in St Ives, she would find him.

Her room was at the top of a steep wooden staircase, but the effort of getting there was worth it when she saw the view. Mike hadn't exaggerated. Below her window, tables and benches were arranged on the pub's cobbled frontage. She had an unrestricted view of the entire bay, all the way from the lifeboat slipway to the harbour wall.

She opened the window to let in the sounds of the seafront, and then lay down on the bed. She needed to think. She'd been up since five that morning and it was now late afternoon. The mattress was soft and she sank into it, watching the dancing patterns the reflections from the sea were making on the ceiling. The sounds of children playing on the beach drifted through the open window and she could hear the occasional clink of glasses from the patio below. Somewhere outside, waves were lapping onto the shore. She closed her eyes.

It was dusk when she woke up, roused by someone tapping on her door. She went to open it, rubbing her eyes. Mike the barman was smiling at her apologetically.

'Sorry to bother you. It's just that we're pretty booked up in the dining room tonight, so if you were planning on coming down for a meal . . . '

Jenna pushed her fingers through her hair. She felt grubby and lethargic. The thought of showering and changing and going downstairs on her own into a dining room full of strangers didn't appeal.

'Would it be too much trouble to have something sent up to my room?'

Mike had apparently anticipated her request and had brought the menu. 'Choose what you like, Miss. I can recommend the roast chicken tonight.'

Jenna told him that sounded just fine,

and asked for a pot of coffee to accompany it. Her meal arrived twenty minutes later. Mike had been right. The chicken was delicious, and the freshly brewed coffee made her feel wide-awake again. If this was a sample of the Harbour Inn's hospitality, then she was going to enjoy her time here.

She stretched and moved to the window. She must have been asleep for hours, because it was completely dark now; all along the seafront, fairy lights twinkled. Reaching for her jacket, she went downstairs and through the busy bar into the street. Everywhere she looked, couples were strolling arm in arm. Many nodded friendly greetings as they passed. Jenna walked to the far side of the harbour from where she could see the entire black curve of the bay. The tide was in and boats clinked at their moorings. She sat on the low harbour wall, disturbing a seagull. It made a chuntering complaint and sidestepped away.

She smiled after it, looking up to gaze

at the canopy of stars. She wondered what it would be like to sit here with Gil Ryder on a night such as this. Suddenly she was feeling very lonely again.

4

Jenna woke with a start next morning to the raucous cries of the gulls. She screwed her eyes closed, listening for the hum of the London traffic, but all she could hear were the noisy birds and the clinking of boats in the harbour. She got up and pulled back the curtains. Early-rising holidaymakers were already out and about, strolling along the water-front, stopping to chat with the local fishermen.

Her mobile trilled and she reached for her bag, hoping it was Gil. But it was her father's name on the caller ID screen.

'Hi, Dad,' she answered. 'You're an early bird.'

'Not that early. It's almost nine.'

'It can't be!' Jenna struggled to grab her watch from the bedside table. It was ten to nine. She'd planned to make an early start today in her quest to find Joss. He'd been careful to always ring Francine from a call box, so she had no mobile number for him.

'Why are you ringing, Dad? Has something happened?'

'Do I need an excuse to call my daughter? Molly told me you'd gone to Cornwall. I just wanted to know how you're getting on down there. Have you found the prodigal son yet?'

Jenna had dragged her case onto the bed and was rummaging with her free hand for something to wear. At home, her outfit would have been laid out from the night before. She was already letting her standards slide.

'If you're referring to Joss, then no. I've only just got here.'

'Well, I shouldn't fret too much about finding him, Jenna. He's a bit of a rascal, taking off like that and leaving his poor wife and kiddies.'

'Like you left me at Fenfleet after Mum died?' The bitter words were out before she had time to stop them.

There was a pause, and then her father said, 'Yes, just like that. Maybe our Joss is more like me than I gave him credit for.'

'Sorry, Dad. You know I didn't mean that. I loved being at Fenfleet.'

Daniel Maitland sighed. 'And I dragged you away from all that to run my little gallery. Now that's what I call selfish.'

Jenna laughed. 'I can see the tongue stuck in your cheek from here. Remorse doesn't suit you, Daniel Maitland. You're up to something.'

When her father was in this kind of mood, it usually meant he'd found a new woman. Romantic attachments featured prominently in her father's life. They only ever lasted long enough for the lady's patience to give out. Jenna adored her father; but he was an artist, with an artist's temperament, and — apart from her mother — she'd never met the woman who could tame him.

'You have a very suspicious mind,

daughter. I'm just saying it's not necessary for you to stay in London, looking after my dusty old gallery. That's what I employ Claire for. You should spread your wings ... enjoy yourself more.'

She could picture him in his studio at the back of the gallery, in his paint-spattered jeans and the faded blue smock he wore to work in. Claire would be out the front in her immaculate dark business suit, checking the clock to make sure the gallery doors would be unlocked precisely on the stroke of nine o'clock.

'I've been indulging in a bit of nostalgia,' he went on, and Jenna heard him sigh. 'Remembering all those lovely holidays we had in Cornwall with Mum.'

Jenna's mind went back again to the little cottage overlooking the harbour ... Daniel hiring a boat ... the two of them out fishing for mackerel.

'I haven't forgotten, Dad,' she said softly.

There was a pause before he came back, but Jenna hadn't missed the little catch in his voice. Despite the succession of female admirers, she knew how much he still missed her mother.

'Well, don't you forget to relax down there, that's all I'm saying. Take some time to enjoy yourself. And, Jenna, if you do manage to find Joss, then just treat it as a bonus.'

'Stop fussing, Dad,' she laughed.

'Who's fussing? How was breakfast, by the way? I hope they're feeding you properly in that place.'

'I was just on my way down to the dining room when you rang,' she lied, frowning at her dishevelled image in the wardrobe mirror.

'I won't keep you, then; but remember, love . . . just enjoy it.'

'I will, I promise.' She smiled at the phone as she clicked it off.

He was right. She was in Cornwall, and she didn't need Gil Ryder's company to enjoy herself. Turning, she stared at the clothes she had pulled from her case. She hadn't exactly packed a business suit, but the things she had put in were definitely on the formal side. She'd stick out like a sore thumb if she wore any of these outfits on the front at St Ives. What had she been thinking?

She went to the window and looked out. It was a parade of whites and pastels, with an occasional touch of navy. She needed a new wardrobe, and that meant an emergency shopping trip to Truro.

By the time she had showered, slipped into a light blue-and-white dress and applied some make-up, she was feeling like a new woman. She was last down for breakfast, but no one seemed to mind. She was beginning to enjoy the relaxing lifestyle in this part of the world. The dining room was small, and although it was bright and sunny this morning, Jenna could imagine the evening atmosphere when the little red candles on the tables cast an intimate glow. An image of Gil's handsome face flitted briefly through her mind again. Annoyed, she forced herself to stop thinking about him. It was becoming a habit, and she had no intention of mooning over a man who clearly wasn't bothered whether he was with her or not.

Breakfasts at the Harbour Inn were hearty affairs, and Jenna surprised herself by polishing off her enormous plate of scrambled eggs and bacon before going to find the hire car she'd asked Mike to organize for her.

The road to Truro was well-signposted, but she checked her map anyway, deciding the most direct route would be along the A30. She'd been told it wasn't the most scenic drive; but it was a shopping trip, after all, and not a sightseeing tour.

Finding a car park in the centre of Truro was no problem, and Jenna was soon wandering around the shops. By noon, she had purchased two pairs of jeans, white shorts and a selection of pastel tops. She even treated herself to a green silk dress and wrap that brought out the green flecks in her hazel eyes. As an afterthought, she added a pair of strappy cream sandals.

Laden with bags, she headed back to her car to stow her purchases safely in the boot. She had intended on driving straight back to St Ives when she'd finished her shopping, and beginning to ask questions about Joss, but she didn't have a clue where to start. She needed a plan. Maybe, if she had another wander around, she might think of something.

She set off back into the centre of Truro, following the signs to the Pannier Market. In London, she was a regular shopper at the markets in Portobello Road and Camden Passage. But this local one had a charm all of its own. She roamed the aisles, enjoying this new carefree feeling, and stopped to browse at a music stall.

She was examining a CD of Cornish fishermen's music, and wondering if her father would like it, when a voice over her shoulder said, 'I didn't have you down as a sea shanty girl.'

Jenna spun round and her eyes widened as she stared into Gil Ryder's smiling face. This couldn't be a coincidence. Had he been in St Ives watching for her, and followed her to Truro? She dismissed the thought as ridiculous as soon as it occurred to her. Yet he *was* here. Her heart began to pound. She tried to ignore it.

'What are you doing here?' she asked, her eyes narrowing.

'Would you believe I'm a tourist?'

'No,' she said, still suspicious.

'What if I said I was here to excavate one of those old stone circles they have so many of in Cornwall?'

She shook her head firmly, struggling to suppress a giggle.

'OK,' he said, holding his hands up in surrender. 'I've been rumbled. The truth is, I've come to keep an eye on you.'

His brown eyes had become serious as he held her gaze. Jenna swallowed. Even if it was true, she hadn't expected such a frank admission.

'What makes you think I need looking after?'

He looked relaxed in light-coloured slacks and a tan suede jacket.

'Maybe I just wanted to see you again,' he said quietly, and then gave her his crooked smile. 'And I feel responsible . . . for your welfare, I mean.'

Jenna frowned. 'So you've been spying on me? You followed me to Truro?' Her voice had risen, annoyance creeping in.

'No. I was joking. This really is a coincidence. I thought you'd still be in St Ives, knocking on doors trying to find Joss.' He checked his watch. 'Look, I know I keep saying this, but it's almost lunchtime. Let's find a nice pub and have a bite to eat.'

'I don't think they do chandeliers in the pubs down here,' Jenna said, keeping a straight face.

'Ouch.' He grinned down at her. 'You really don't take any prisoners, do you, Miss Maitland? But I promise this meal will definitely be more low key than that fancy London bistro.'

Half an hour later, they were sitting on the terrace of a creek-side pub just outside Truro, watching two white herons strut their stuff along the muddy banks opposite. Gil had brought two glasses of local cider from the bar, and they sat enjoying the sun as they waited for their crab salads.

Jenna was reluctant to spoil what was proving to be an even better day than she had imagined, but the questions were still racing around inside her head.

She bit her lip. 'OK, Gil,' she started. 'Do you want to tell me what's really going on?'

'Huh?'

'Well try this for starters,' she went on, picking up her cutlery as their food arrived. 'You come into the gallery on the pretext of buying a painting.'

'It wasn't a pretext,' he interrupted. 'It was a present for Caroline.'

'You haven't answered my question.'

'I thought I had. I told you the other

day that I wanted to help find Joss. I knew all about you before we met. Molly and Isaac were always singing your praises.' He shrugged. 'I was intrigued. I suppose I wanted to check you out before I revealed myself, so to speak.'

She gave him a suspicious look. 'And are you still checking up on me?'

He leaned forward, meeting her wide-eyed gaze. Her heart was hammering again.

'There's nothing sinister in my wanting to be here with you, Jenna,' he said, his eyes serious. 'Meeting you in Truro today really was a coincidence, you know. And, just for the record, I definitely wasn't following you.'

She coloured. 'I'm sorry . . . I didn't mean . . . '

He reached for her hand, but she couldn't bring herself to meet his eyes. For a few seconds, neither of them spoke, and then Gil cleared his throat.

'Now eat that salad,' he ordered.

For a split second her eyes flashed

anger, then she realized he was teasing her. She gave him an embarrassed grin and picked up her cutlery. 'This looks great,' she said. 'How did you know I was starving?'

Ten minutes later, when she had cleared every morsel from her plate, she licked her fingers and reached for a paper napkin. 'The Cornish air must be giving me an appetite,' she said, patting her tummy. 'I'll have to cut the calories when I get back to London.'

'I hope you don't,' he said, quietly. 'I happen to think you look pretty wonderful just as you are.'

Jenna's heart did a somersault, but when she dared to look up at him it was as though he had never uttered the compliment. His brow had creased in a way that was becoming familiar, and she followed his stare out across the creek. The ferry carrying passengers from Falmouth to Truro had just come into view, and they watched as it sailed past.

'Look,' he said, pointing to the bank

opposite. 'The herons have come back.'

Jenna peered but saw nothing. Gil scraped back his chair and came to stand behind her. He bent down, taking her head in his hands, cradling it towards the feeding birds. He was so close that she caught the faint smell of his aftershave, and something inside her leapt.

'Just there,' he said, his voice gentle. 'Can you see them?'

She wasn't looking. She'd closed her eyes, savouring the sensation of his fingers cool on her cheeks. Without warning, he stood up again and went back to his chair. The intimate moment had gone. They sat staring at the water. The silence between them was deafening, and she knew that Gil had felt that same connection.

She swallowed, and said, 'I get the feeling you've been here before.'

He nodded, the tension between them easing. 'My folks have a house down here.' He smiled, holding her gaze. 'It's a kind of bolthole. It's quite isolated and difficult to get to, but it's worth the effort. I've never found a better place to relax.'

It was the first time he had mentioned his parents. She tried to picture their family holidays in the isolated cottage. An image flashed through her mind of the young Gil in short trousers, knees scraped from climbing trees, dark hair flopping over a grubby, laughing face. She wanted to know everything about those days, everything about him, but he didn't seem inclined to tell her any more. She sensed that if she tried to probe further then the shutters would come down. This obviously wasn't the time. She could wait.

Instead, she said, 'I think I mentioned I used to come here on holiday with my parents too. Mum loved Cornwall. She and Dad rented this tiny cottage right by the harbour in Polperro.' Memories were racing back, and she looked up to find him watching her.

'Happy times?'

She smiled. 'They were glorious days. Dad taught me to fish with a line from a rowing boat.' Her eyes were shining. 'I was pretty good at it, as I remember. We would come back with a bagful of mackerel and Mum would cook them for tea.'

Gil pushed his empty plate aside and leaned forward. 'Polperro isn't too far away,' he said. 'We could take a run out there . . . maybe even find that cottage.'

Her eyes widened. 'Go back to Polperro?' She hadn't thought about doing that during her time in Cornwall, but she had to admit that it would be nice.

'What about my hire car? It's still in Truro.'

'Not a problem. We can call in there and check on the parking arrangements, then I'll drop you back at it on the way home.' He had it all thought out.

Jenna nodded her agreement, and once they'd made sure that her hire car would come to no harm, they set off for the coast. Gil was a confident driver, but she sensed their sedate pace was for her benefit, for she knew how fast his powerful sports car could really travel. The roads were busy and the trip took longer than she had expected. It was late afternoon when they parked at the top of the village then walked down the steep hill to the harbour.

'Any of this starting to look familiar?' he asked as they reached the little bridge at the heart of the village.

'I remember all of it,' she said, her excitement mounting as she spotted their holiday cottage across the harbour. 'Dad and I used to sit here for hours, watching all the little boats come and go. Look!' She pointed. 'That was our place.'

Gil looked across to the row of whitewashed fishermen's dwellings.

'I can see Mum now, waving at us from that little window, calling us in for tea.' Her voice trailed off, and Gil saw her wipe away a tear. He resisted the urge to take her in his arms.

'I'm sorry,' he said, gently. 'I shouldn't have suggested this. It's upsetting you.'

'No. I'm not upset, just feeling a bit nostalgic. Mum died when I was ten, and all this . . . ' She flicked a hand around the scene. 'Well, it just brings it all back.'

They wandered around the village, and Gil bought Jenna a tiny Cornish Piskie in one of the gift shops.

'For luck,' he said, smiling, folding it into her hand.

Jenna clasped the silver trinket to her chest. 'I'll treasure it forever,' she laughed.

'You better had,' he said, trying to sound stern. 'It cost the best part of a fiver.'

It felt good walking beside him. He didn't seem to notice the admiring glances that sometimes strayed in his direction from passing women.

'Is your father a good artist?' he suddenly asked.

His question took her by surprise, and she frowned. 'Not just good, but famous. I'm surprised you haven't heard of Daniel Maitland.'

'I have, actually,' Gil said, 'I thought perhaps that was why he brought you to Cornwall for holidays . . . you know, plenty of picturesque harbours, pretty cottages, and all those coves to paint.'

'You're right, actually. Dad did paint a lot when we were down here.' She sighed. 'He hoped I would follow in his footsteps, but I'm afraid I don't have his gift.'

'You look artistic enough to me,' he said, grinning down at her.

She swiped a hand at him. 'Stop mocking me. I didn't say I had *no* talent, just not enough to make a living at it. I'm good at selling paintings, just not so hot at actually creating them.'

'So, you turned your attention to running your father's gallery?' he said.

Jenna nodded. 'Now, that is something I actually *can* do better than my father. He says I have the Maitland head for business.'

Gil was thoughtful, but he said nothing.

It was a steep climb back up the hill to Gil's car, so they stopped at a pink-painted tearoom and ordered cream teas.

'I really will go home tons heavier,' Jenna wailed, eyeing the pots of clotted cream and strawberry jam that came with the freshly-baked scones.

'You can't come to Cornwall and not have a cream tea,' he scolded.

'Alright, I'll eat it,' she laughed, 'but you might have to carry me up that hill to the car.'

'That can be arranged,' he said, his eyes teasing.

They had relaxed in each other's company. Maybe this was her chance to find out a bit more about him.

'Are your parents staying here in their holiday cottage at the moment?' she asked.

He frowned, but he hadn't growled at her, so she went on. 'You don't talk much about them.'

'I don't want to bore you.'

His expression was closed, and she wondered if he was warning her off. For whatever reason, Gil seemed determined not to talk, and she tried to dismiss the nagging doubt that there could be another reason why he wanted to be in Cornwall. She didn't want to think about that. Why shouldn't he have offered to bring her, simply because he enjoyed her company?

They'd arrived back at his car and she said, 'Are we working together to find Joss now? Is that the plan?'

'If that's what you want.'

Jenna frowned. She wasn't sure that it was. She had a feeling that she'd have more chance of persuading Joss to return home if Gil wasn't with her.

'Let's just see what tomorrow brings,' she said quietly, getting into the car.

They drove back to Truro in companionable silence, and Jenna's head sank back into the expensive green upholstery as a winsome smile played on her lips.

Gil glanced across at her and grinned. 'Tired?'

'Hmm, a bit,' she said, studying his handsome profile. 'I've had a lovely day, Gil. Thank you.'

'It doesn't have to be over yet. It's early. Let's find somewhere to have supper.'

She shook her head. 'Thanks, but I really need to get back to St Ives. So if you don't mind just dropping me off at my car . . . '

He frowned and glanced back at her. 'Sure I can't persuade you?'

Her heart gave a mighty flip. It was a tempting offer. But she mustered all her willpower and turned to him. 'No, really. I should get back. If I'm to find Joss, then I have a lot of detective work to do, and for that I need an early night.'

Jenna thought she saw the ghost of a smile flicker at the corners of Gil's mouth.

'Good for you,' he said.

By the time she was back behind the

wheel of her hire car and driving to the pub, the lovely afternoon had mellowed into a fine evening. The road was quiet, and she went over the day's events in her mind. Gil Ryder was like no other man she had ever met. She found herself wondering about his parents' cottage, and if he was returning there at that moment. He hadn't even told her where in Cornwall it was. In fact, he hadn't told her anything. She'd spent the best part of a day with him, and she knew no more about the man than she had on the morning he'd walked into her father's gallery.

5

It was just after eight when Jenna arrived back at the Harbour Inn, and the buzz of voices as she came through the bar with her collection of carrier bags told her that business was in full swing. Mike caught her eye and waved what she assumed to be a menu at her, so she mouthed 'No thanks' and carried on. She'd eaten enough for one day. But he hurried after her and thrust a letter into her hand.

'This came for you, Jenna,' he said breathlessly.

She stared down at her name on the envelope, thinking the handwriting was familiar. As far as she was aware, only Gil and her father knew she was staying here. She could feel her heartbeat quicken as she ran upstairs, dumped her bags on the bed, and stood studying the envelope. She hardly dare open it, but she had to know if her suspicion was right. She tore the envelope apart and the words all but jumped from the page.

Jenna, what on earth are you doing here? I suppose my parents sent you. I can't imagine it would have been Francine. Well, your journey has been in vain, because I'm not going home, although it would be nice to see a friendly face (if you and I are still friends, that is). So if you're passing my way in the morning, feel free to drop in. You can find me at Seagull Cottage.

Joss.

P.S. If you take the road up to the Tate, my cottage is on your right. You can't miss it.

Jenna clutched the letter to her chest, feeling like dancing round the room. She'd done it! She'd found Joss . . . but there had been no mention of any woman. She studied the note again, turning it over. Her first instinct was to rush out and find this Seagull Cottage. She'd already wasted a day . . . But a voice inside her head was counselling her to wait. Joss would be expecting her in the morning, and the last thing she wanted was to antagonize him. She'd do things his way. She'd be patient.

The evening had become overcast and a fine mist was creeping in from the sea. From her window, she could see people still strolling along the front, their only concessions to the worsening weather being long-sleeved tops and light jackets. The clothes she'd bought in Truro were still in their shiny bags, so she clicked on the bedside light and began to put them away. The bright, summery colours had matched her mood when she close them. She glanced back to the window. The sky was getting darker, and she guessed rain was not far away.

Joss's note lay on the bed, and she

picked it up again, glancing once more through his directions. *Take the road up to the Tate.* She supposed he meant the Tate Art Gallery. It was on her mental list of places not to be missed while she was in Cornwall. She'd seen pictures of the spectacular white gallery, built into the cliff-face overlooking a popular surfing beach on the other side of the town. If she had time, she'd definitely pay a visit. Maybe Joss would take her?

She had promised Daniel a daily update, so reached for the mobile phone in her bag. As she did, the tiny black box containing Gil's lucky Cornish Piskie fell out. Retrieving it, she opened the box and tipped the silver trinket into the palm of her hand, gazing at it until she felt the prick of tears. It had been one of the best days of her life. They had made no plans to meet again, but Jenna knew they would. She was sure she hadn't imagined that look in Gil's eyes as he watched her drive away. Her fingers closed over the charm, enjoying the feel of it in her hand.

She picked up her mobile, and listened as her father's phone rang for a few seconds before it was answered.

'Hi Dad,' she called.

'Jenna!' She could hear the smile in his voice. 'How's Cornwall?'

'Just as beautiful as ever.'

'Have you found my wayward nephew yet?'

'I have, actually.' She told him about Joss's note.

Daniel sighed. 'I suppose that's good news, but steady as you go, girl. Remember, you can't make him go home if he doesn't want to.' There was a pause, and then Daniel asked, 'So what happens now? Have you told Isaac and Molly?

'Not yet. I don't want to give them any false hopes. I'll ring them after I see Joss. Maybe by then I'll know a bit more about what's going on.'

'Good plan,' Daniel said. 'If the family asked you to do this, then I'm

sure they will trust your judgment.'
There was a hesitation. 'On the other
hand, it might put their minds at rest if
you just told them he's contacted you.'

Jenna bit her lip. She wasn't sure
now. Maybe she should ring Gil and ask
his advice about Joss's letter? But a
little voice in her head still told her to
wait.

'I think I'll hang on until tomorrow,
Dad.'

She could hear him sighing again at
the other end of the phone. 'I'm sure
you know best, my darling, but just
don't be too nice to the young
scallywag. He wants a kick up the . . . '

'I get the picture, Dad,' Jenna
interrupted, laughing. Her father had
never been the most diplomatic of men.
To change the subject, she told him
about her visit to Polperro.

'Polperro?' She heard the surprised
inflection in his voice. 'You said
we . . . ?'

The words were out before she'd
realized the implications. Now she

would have to explain about Gil.

'Er . . . Gil Ryder took me.'

'Gil . . . ?' Daniel repeated the name slowly, and Jenna thought he was trying to remember where he had heard it before. Then he said, 'Isaac's sidekick . . . the one who came to the gallery and bought the print? Oh, yes, I delivered it to his sister yesterday.'

It was Jenna's turn to be surprised. '*You* delivered it? I thought we paid a courier service for that?'

'Well, I was passing that way,' her father said, breezily, then continued, 'You were telling me about Mr Ryder.'

Jenna nodded at the phone. 'He drove me down here, and then we met up in Truro this morning. His parents have a holiday cottage. When I mentioned our family holidays in Polperro, he insisted on taking me back there.' She knew she was rattling on, sounding defensive. Her father was unlikely to miss that.

'Sounds like you're quite taken with this young man.'

'No, not especially,' she lied. 'He knows Joss, and he gave me a lift to Cornwall because he wants to help the family.'

'How does taking you to Polperro help the family?'

'Look, Dad, I'm a big girl now. I can look after myself. Besides, Gil's a nice man — and I trust him.'

'Fair enough, Jenna. I'm sure you know what you're doing. Just be careful, that's all I'm saying . . . and keep in touch.'

The call had unnerved her. Her father was no fool, and he obviously suspected Gil was not being straight with her. She wondered if it was something his sister Caroline had said when the picture was delivered. Was she allowing a handsome, charismatic man to turn her head? Surely she wasn't that naive? But one thing was certain: whether she wanted to or not, she was becoming more and more attracted to Gil Ryder.

Jenna slept fitfully that night, dreaming of fairy goblins casting magic dust over her bed. It was the silence that woke her. She missed the sounds of London, the constant hum of traffic, the early morning flights from Heathrow. It was still dark when she slipped out of bed and went to the window to draw back the curtains. The mist had cleared and the moon was casting a silvery path on the water. Out over the sea, a solitary gull sent up a forlorn cry. She shuddered. Somewhere out there, maybe even not very far away, Gil would be sleeping. She imagined his dark head on a pillow, a tanned arm flung out across the sheets. She crept back to bed, smiling, and pulled up the duvet.

Next morning, she woke with a start — something was moving across the roof above her bed. She listened as the pattering noises quickened, then sank back onto her pillow with a relieved smile. It was a bird, probably a seagull, running across the tiles above her little bay window. If she stayed in St Ives long enough, she'd get used to stuff like this. She sat up and stretched, throwing back the duvet, and went to check the weather. Last night's shimmering moon-light had been replaced by the glare of early-morning sunshine, glinting on the sea. The harbour and quayside were already buzzing with activity, and a number of small fishing boats drifted out in the bay.

Her meeting with Joss might take some careful handling. As she showered and dressed in her new jeans and a white T-shirt she'd bought in Truro, she planned her strategy . . . friendly, but firm. But what if Francine was right and he was living with someone? She had no strategy for that. She ran a brush through her glossy dark hair, and stared at the unfamiliar image in the mirror. She would never have left her London flat looking like this. Her clothes would have been co-ordinated, smart and chic, with matching high-heeled shoes to counteract her barely-five-feet-four-inches height. And she would have spent at least fifteen minutes on her make-up, for you never knew who might walk into the gallery.

Thinking of the gallery brought back the memory of the first time she'd seen Gil, and a tingling sensation surged through her. She'd buy a silver chain today, and wear his lucky charm around her neck.

It was almost ten o'clock as she strolled along the front, enjoying the warm summer sun on her face. The tourists had also finished their breakfasts and were emerging from their guesthouses, filtering into the gift shops, setting up deckchairs for their day on the beach. Joss hadn't specified a time when he'd be home, but time didn't seem to matter down here. A boatman at the harbour pointed her in the direction of the Tate, and she set off, checking the names of cottages on the way.

Seagull Cottage, when she eventually found it, was a shock. Jenna had been expecting something similar to the other pretty dwellings she'd passed. She'd imagined a quaint little house with a low roof, whitewashed walls and a brightly-painted front door. But Seagull Cottage was nothing like that. It was three floors high, and the faded blue door, halfway up its grey stone frontage, was reached by a flight of stone steps that ran flush with the building. The rusty rail didn't look safe, so Jenna avoided it as she climbed up.

The door opened before she could raise her hand to knock, and Joss, in frayed denim shorts and a grubby T-shirt, bare-footed and with a frying pan in his hand, stepped aside for her to enter.

'Saw you coming.' He scowled. 'You're late.'

She stared at the frying pan and his general demeanour, which suggested he had only just got up, and swept past him into the cottage. 'OK,' she announced, throwing up her hands in a gesture of defiance. 'You can tell me to mind my own business if you want, but if I was going to do that I wouldn't be here.'

Joss shook his head and frowned after her as she marched ahead of him into his untidy kitchen. 'Pleased to see you, too, cousin dear,' he muttered, following her through.

It wasn't the reception she'd been expecting. Where was the cheeky grin, or the teasing blue eyes? Where was the friendly greeting? He was treating her as though she were the enemy.

She pulled out a chair and sat down at a chipped wooden table, glancing at the chaos around her. The sink was full of dirty dishes; beside it was an opened tin of baked beans, the jagged lid sticking up.

He followed her gaze and saw what she saw. 'OK, it's a pit,' he said. 'But it's all mine.'

She wanted to ask what he was doing here . . . why he was living like this . . . and why there was no sign of the mysterious woman. But she merely shrugged. 'I didn't say a word.'

He gave her an irritated grimace and went back to his cooking. Jenna stared at his back as he broke eggs into a frying pan. Even in these tatty clothes he had arrogance, an air of confidence that didn't fit these surroundings. She was beginning to suspect that the unkempt appearance of both his cottage and himself had been quite deliberate. But why? Within minutes he had produced a plate of sausages, eggs and bacon and clattered it down on the table between a knife and fork.

'I'm guessing you've already eaten,' he said, settling himself to his meal.

Jenna eyed the food and nodded. At least he wasn't starving himself. She sat in silence, waiting for him to finish, and then decided she could make herself useful. 'Where do you keep the coffee?'

Joss nodded at a cupboard and she took out the things she needed, surprised that it was filter and not instant. When it was made she passed him a mug and sat opposite.

'What's going on, Joss? This isn't like you.'

He looked up, fixing her with his

intense stare, but his voice was brusque. 'Oh, you know what I'm like, do you, Jenna? Well, that's very clever of you, because even I don't know that.'

'Francine is going out of her mind with worry — not to mention what Molly and Isaac are going though. Couldn't you at least call them and tell them you're OK?'

He ran his fingers through his hair. 'It's not that easy. You don't know what it's been like for me those last few months. I was never made to run a business. I think Mum understands that, but Dad never will. So I said nothing and went along with it all. I did everything that was expected of me. I wore the suit, drove the smart car, attended the business meetings. No one ever considered what I wanted.' He glanced at the collection of paint-brushes crammed into a jar on the windowsill. 'Over the past year, Dad has been grooming me to take over the company. I can't do that, Jenna. I can't live my father's life for him. I don't want to run an empire. I only want to paint.'

Jenna's mind went back to the time when Isaac had put Joss in charge of the Harrogate store. He had charmed both customers and staff. Under his charge, the profits had increased. Joss was a natural businessman, but if he wanted to pretend otherwise, then she would have to go along with it — for the moment anyway.

Jenna cleared her throat. 'I understand what you're saying, Joss, but what about Francine and Charlotte and Alfie? How confusing must it be for tiny three-year-olds to understand why their daddy doesn't come home anymore!'

Joss looked away, and Jenna knew he was hiding a tear. 'Francine doesn't want me back. She's said so.'

'She's hurt, Joss.' Jenna hesitated, but she had to bring it up. 'She thinks you've left her for another woman.'

Joss stared at her. 'She thinks what? There's no other woman! Why would she think that?'

'She was seen getting into your Jeep the day you left Fenfleet. You kissed her, for heaven's sake.'

He shook his head, trying to make sense of what he was hearing. Then realization dawned. 'Victoria! I gave Victoria a lift. She said she had a friend down here, and asked if I could take her with me.' He nodded, remembering. 'She did kiss me, but it was a thank-you for giving her a lift.'

He saw Jenna's eyebrow lift. 'There's nothing going on between me and Victoria. Heaven forbid! I felt sorry for her, that's all.'

'Is she still here?'

'I've no idea. But, by way of saying thank-you, she insisted on posing for me. I didn't see her after that first week, so I assumed she'd gone back to Yorkshire.'

Jenna sank back in her chair. She believed him. Giving a lift to someone in trouble was exactly the kind of thing Joss would do. And besides, there was no sign of anyone else sharing his apparently chaotic living arrangements.

'You have to tell Francine about this. You have to call her, Joss.'

He shifted uncomfortably in his chair. 'I know . . . I can't have her thinking that.' He looked up, and Jenna could see the confusion in his eyes. 'But if I make things right with Francine she'll want me to go back.'

'Would that be so awful?'

'I'm not ready to do that . . . not yet. I have to sort things out in my head first.'

Jenna said nothing, hoping the silence would encourage him to go on.

He jumped up suddenly, beckoning for her to follow him into a little sitting room. There was a painting above the fireplace and she went to study it. Joss had captured the drama of its stormy scene, a fishing boat riding the waves, with the sea creaming at its hull. The image was so real that Jenna could imagine the crew's desperate battle to keep their vessel powering through the squall. She stood back, engrossed in the work. Catching such a moment on canvas took real talent.

'Well, what's the verdict?' he asked.

Jenna was still studying the painting. It was remarkably good.

'I think it's wonderful, Joss.'

He looked away, embarrassed. But she turned him back to face her. 'OK, so you have talent. We've always known that. But I still don't understand why you had to take off like that.'

'My parents don't think I have any artistic talent. They see all this as a waste of time.'

'Have you ever shown them your work?'

Joss's shoulders rose in a shrug. 'No point. I know what they would say.'

Jenna gave an exasperated sigh.

'You always were stubborn. Has anyone seen your work?'

'I don't show it around, if that's what you're asking.'

'Does that mean you won't let me see what else you've painted?'

She thought at first that he would

refuse, but he didn't. He turned, beckoning her to follow him through the cottage to the room he used as a studio.

Light flooded in through sliding glass doors, and outside she could see a small balcony with a view over the rooftops to the harbour. It had obviously been intended as the cottage's sitting room, but she could understand why he had chosen to paint here.

Several more canvases in various stages of completion were stacked against the far away wall. There was an easel in the middle of the room with his current work in progress, which seemed to be of a gaunt wooden structure on a desolate clifftop with a wild sea churning in the background. It wasn't a painting to be ignored.

'I can't understand why you want to keep all this to yourself. People should see these, Joss.'

'You wouldn't be trying to drum up business for that gallery of yours?'

'Well, that would be up to you. Any

of these canvases would be good enough to exhibit. You should think about it.'

He glanced over to the stacked paintings and scratched his head, releasing a long, painful sigh. 'Oh, I don't know, Jenna. My life feels like such a mess at the moment.'

'You should go home, Joss. Speak to Isaac. Tell him how you feel. He'll understand. You're more important to him than any business.'

But he shook his head. 'You don't understand. It's expected of me to run the business. The family sees it as my duty. If I refuse, then the company will have to be sold to strangers. That would kill my parents. Don't you see, Jenna? It's all down to me — and I just can't deal with that right now.'

As she turned to go, she spotted another, smaller canvas in the corner. 'That's Victoria,' Joss said, following her gaze.

The girl was beautiful. He'd painted her on a clifftop, her long blonde hair streaked back by the wind, green eyes glinting defiance. 'How do you know her?'

Joss came to stand beside her. 'Oh, didn't I say? She's Gil Ryder's girl-friend.'

Jenna's heart missed a beat. Had she heard right? Why hadn't he told her? Was this what her father had learned from Caroline? Suddenly, she needed to be alone.

But, as she turned to go, Joss caught her wrist. 'Thanks for coming, Jenna.' He hesitated for a second. 'You can ring Fenfleet, if you like. Tell them I'm fine.'

She turned to face him, and he was smiling. His whole demeanour was suddenly different, more relaxed. She nodded. 'I'll tell them. But I'm coming back tomorrow, Joss. You and I have more to talk about.'

A sudden thought struck her as she headed for the door, and she spun round, frowning. 'How did you know, by the way, that I was in Cornwall and staying down by the harbour?'

Joss lifted an eyebrow. 'Because this is St Ives.' He grinned. 'And my spies are everywhere.'

6

Pacing her room, Jenna thought hard, trying to work out just what Gil was up to. He hadn't told her he was involved with anyone, but then he hadn't said he wasn't. She'd just assumed that. She snatched up a pillow from the bed and thumped at it. How could she have been so stupid as to fall for the charms of a stranger? She was too angry with herself to cry. When she considered it, she realized that any connection she'd felt between them must have been in her own head after all. Her father had known this all along and tried to warn her, but she'd been too headstrong to see it.

Another thought was beginning to creep into her mind, one she liked even less. What if Gil had been using her to find this Victoria? Maybe he already knew that she'd left Yorkshire with Joss.

The same man who'd given the information to Francine could also have told Gil.

A shiver ran down her spine. She didn't like being used. Her head was spinning. She was remembering the beautiful girl in Joss's painting. Was Gil with her now? It was too painful to even think about. She must forget about Gil Ryder and concentrate instead on the reason she was here. Things had gone well with Joss, and she would see him again in the morning.

She rang her father and recounted the meeting, telling him about the paintings Joss had produced in Cornwall. 'Some of them reminded me of your work, Dad.'

There was a moment's silence at the other end of the line, and then Daniel said, 'The lad's got talent, then?'

'I would say so. If things work out, you could offer him an exhibition at the gallery.'

'That good, eh? Well, we'll have to see about that. Have you told Molly and

Isaac that you've found the lad?'

'Not yet. It's complicated.'

'Then uncomplicate it, Jenna. All they want to know right now is that their boy is safe and well. Leave out the other stuff for the moment. Will you do that?'

She sighed into the phone. 'You're right, Dad.'

'That's because I'm a wise old man who, right now, needs to be somewhere else. Rupert will already be setting up the board at our table in the pub — and I know that old rogue's not above cheating.'

Rupert Fox was the proprietor of an antiques shop near the gallery, but he seemed to spend most of his time drinking coffee in Daniel's studio. Jenna smiled, remembering the two old friends' weekly chess game in the nearby Red Lion. It all sounded so comfortingly normal.

' . . . and don't forget to give Molly and Isaac my love when you speak to them,' Daniel concluded.

'I won't. Thanks, Dad.'

Jenna knew she had been putting off ringing the Maitlands. She'd no idea why she was nervous about it, because her meeting with Joss had gone well. And at least she could tell them he was fine. It was Isaac who answered the phone.

'Any news?'

She could hear the anxiety in his voice. 'Yes,' she said, 'And it's good. I found Joss and went to see him this morning.'

There was a sharp intake of breath at the other end of the line, and then Isaac said, 'Thank God. Where is he?'

Jenna told him and described her meeting with her cousin. 'Joss is painting quite a lot. He showed me some of his canvases. They're really good, Isaac.'

'Is he coming home?' His voice was strained. He didn't sound well.

'Not yet, but I'm hopeful.'

She could hear the click of Molly's heels crossing the wooden floor.

'Is that you, Jenna? Isaac says you've found Joss!'

She repeated the morning's events, knowing Molly was hanging on to every word.

'Have you spoken to Francine?' Molly asked.

'No, Joss wanted to do that himself. It's best to let them sort things out for themselves now, don't you think?'

She signed off, with Molly's words of gratitude still ringing in her ears.

The small bedroom was beginning to feel claustrophobic. Her head was pounding and she had to get out of there. The buzz of the busy bar reached her as she came down the stairs. Mike, with two other young barmen she hadn't seen before, was working at full stretch pulling pints and pouring drinks for thirsty customers. Waitresses, still amazingly cheerful, nodded to her as they squeezed past, delivering bar meals to the crowded tables.

'What's the celebration, Mike?' she called over the surrounding babble.

'This is just our usual lunchtime trade,' he grinned, placing the half-pint of cider she'd ordered on the bar in front of her. 'Most of them are visitors just celebrating being in Cornwall.'

Jenna thought of the London pubs where she often had to meet clients. None of them were anything like this. She would miss St Ives when she went home. Glancing round, she could see there was no chance of a seat indoors.

She picked up her cider and began to make her way outside; but, if anything, it was even busier out here. She turned to go back inside when a voice at her shoulder demanded, 'What do you want with Gil?'

Jenna spun round and found herself staring into a pair of venomous green eyes. The girl's fair skin was tanned golden, and her long blonde hair had been plaited into a single rope. So this was Victoria!

'I don't know why you're here,' she hissed, advancing on Jenna, 'but you stay away from Gil . . . he's spoken for!'

The little scene would have been menacing if it hadn't been so ridiculous.

'I'm warning you,' she snarled. 'Stay away from him!'

Jenna was aware of the curious looks they were attracting from other customers. Out of the corner of her eye she could see people whispering and looking in their direction. Victoria turned to go, satisfied that her message had been delivered, but Jenna caught her arm. She wasn't going to leave it like this.

'I think you and I need to talk,' she said firmly, thumping down her glass and nodding towards the beach. 'Let's take a walk?'

The tide had receded, uncovering the heavy chains the boatmen used to tether their vessels. When they were out of hearing of the sunbathers on the beach, Jenna swung round angrily to the woman. 'I didn't catch your name.'

'Victoria Symington.' The girl's chin lifted in a gesture of defiance.

'Well, listen up, *Ms* Symington.' Jenna's eyes sparked fire. 'I'll see who I choose, and whenever I choose. But if you're talking about Gil Ryder, then he's here to help me on a . . . on a family matter.'

'Gil never mentioned any 'family matter'.' Victoria's elegant nose lifted in a sneer. 'And he certainly never mentioned *you*. But then again, he didn't have to. You have the Maitland look.'

Jenna's eyes narrowed. 'How did you know I was here with Gil? You just said he'd never mentioned me. I don't believe you've even spoken to him.'

Victoria glanced away, and in that second Jenna knew she had been lying. But if she hadn't met up with Gil, then how did she know they'd arrived together? Then it clicked. 'You've been spying on us!'

The woman's glare was hostile. 'What's the big secret? I saw you two together . . . saw you going in there.' She flicked her head back towards the inn. 'I suppose you're here to talk Joss into going back to Yorkshire. Well, I hope you don't succeed. He just wants the lot of you to leave him alone.'

Jenna had been fighting to keep a lid on her anger, but this girl's audacity was astounding her. 'Now, just a minute,' she cut in. 'Joss and I are cousins. But I'm struggling to see what it has to do with you.'

Victoria's green eyes glinted with malice. 'Joss doesn't want you here — and Gil only came down to Cornwall to see me, so you can stop making eyes at him. Do you understand?' She pushed her face close to Jenna's. 'You're upsetting people . . . and you should go!'

This was ridiculous. Jenna opened her mouth to retaliate, but Victoria had already turned on her heel and was marching off, her long plait swinging.

Jenna's first impulse was to run after her, grab her arm and yell at this outrageous woman that she couldn't be intimidated. But the words *Gil only came down to Cornwall to see me* kept flashing through Jenna's mind. She stared after Victoria, watched her leave the beach, run along the road and turn a corner out of sight. If what she said was true, then Jenna really had been a fool to allow herself to fall under Gil's spell. She turned and wandered along the curve of white sand, keeping close to the water's edge to avoid the deckchairs, striped windbreaks, and all the other paraphernalia that accompanied the families of holidaymakers on the beach.

Her mind kept returning to the painting of Victoria she'd seen in Joss's studio, and an involuntary shiver ran through her. If the woman was telling the truth, then it was no wonder Gil hadn't mentioned where he was staying. He had been with Victoria all along! Jenna's blood was racing. She bent to pick up a pebble and hurled it into the sea, scattering a cluster of black-and-white wading birds that had been foraging at the tidemark.

She couldn't face going back to her

room, squeezing past all those happy holidaymakers in the bar, so she headed for the narrow, winding streets of the town centre. But it wasn't long before the cobbled thoroughfares of St Ives felt as though they were closing in on her, making her feel distinctly claustrophobic. She had to get away.

Her hire car was still parked behind the pub. The thought of driving out of the busy town and into the countryside was suddenly irresistible. As she picked up speed, hurrying back to the Harbour Inn, she could see just ahead that a green low-slung car was attempting to inch its way along the narrow, crowded street. Jenna stepped aside to allow it to pass; as she did so, the driver's window slid down and she found herself staring at a familiar face.

'Well, Jenna.' The driver smiled. 'We meet again.'

Jenna's heart was thudding. Why hadn't she instantly recognized the car? She'd spent enough time in it the previous day. She gaped stupidly at the handsome tanned features and her legs turned to jelly. 'Gil! What are you doing here?'

He glanced around at the milling crowds of jaywalkers, and frowned. 'Possibly making the biggest mistake of my life trying to drive along here.'

Jenna gave a nervous laugh and eyed the elegant sports car. 'Vehicles can be a positive disadvantage in this town, even ones like this.'

'Is that why everyone's looking at me like I was an alien?'

She nodded, wondering why Victoria wasn't sitting next to him in the passenger seat.

'I'd feel a lot more at home if you would have dinner with me tonight.' His mouth had curved into a persuasive grin as she gaped at him. She'd give the man full marks for audacity.

Another car had edged its way through the crowds behind him, and the driver was threatening to give his horn an impatient blast.

'I'll send a car to pick you up. Shall

we say, about seven-thirty?' he called back, as his car pulled slowly away.

Jenna opened her mouth to tell him not to bother ... that she had no intention of having dinner with him. But somehow the words stuck in her throat, and she gave a feeble nod as his hand came out in a wave. She was still shaking as she watched him disappear round a corner at the end of the road.

What was he doing here? Had he come to St Ives hoping to find her? But of course he hadn't. He'd probably come to see Victoria. So why had he invited *her* for dinner again? Jenna's heart was pumping. She took a deep breath, trying to calm the feelings surging through her body. It was ridiculous to feel this excited. It was only dinner.

7

Jenna's head was still spinning as she walked back to the Harbour Inn. Knowing Gil was involved with another woman should have changed everything, but it didn't. This man still had the power to reduce her to a trembling wreck. All afternoon, she'd been going over in her mind how she would deal with seeing him again. She'd play it cool . . . be in control . . . distant even. But one look from those teasing brown eyes, and her resolve had crumbled. And now she'd agreed to spend the evening with him.

Back in her room, she stared down from her window. The tide had crept back since the earlier confrontation with Victoria. Boats were returning to harbour, their owners busy with the business of securing ropes and making their vessels safe for the night. She went over in her mind what Joss had said about Victoria. It hadn't been much, but if he was telling the truth — and she was sure that he was — then he didn't even know she was still in St Ives. Yet he'd brought her all the way to Cornwall with him. Why would he have done that when he knew she was Gil's girlfriend? Jenna wondered if there was more to all this than Joss had told her.

She caught sight of herself in the mirror and frowned. She didn't recognize herself any more. No one would imagine that this wide-eyed, tanned and windswept girl in T-shirt and jeans was the same elegant young businesswoman she'd been only days ago. There was a distinct high-spirited gleam in her large hazel eyes and she wondered what her father would make of the new Jenna.

She sighed; she was sure she'd made a mistake accepting Gil's dinner invitation. What if she turned up and Victoria was with him? She shuddered. By going to him this evening, she could be getting herself into a whole lot of trouble. On the other hand, Gil Ryder owed her an explanation — and that was exactly what she would demand when she saw him again.

The incident with Victoria had shaken her confidence, but she had no intention of skulking off like a scolded schoolgirl. Tonight she would look her best! Tonight she would dazzle! She had nothing to lose — and she would give the smug Victoria Symington a run for her money.

After showering and shampooing the day's dust from her hair, she went to the wardrobe for a critical assessment of her options. The green silk dress and wrap she'd bought in Truro were hanging at the back, and she lifted them out to hold in front of herself. She'd been right about the colour. She dressed quickly and strapped on her new sandals before making a final twirl in front of the mirror. The Cornish sun had given her normally pale skin a pleasing glow.

But as she waited for Gil's car, she

could feel her confidence ebbing again. And when a hire car arrived to collect her, she was almost tempted to send it away — but if she did that, she might never get to the bottom of this. She reminded herself of her promise to Molly and Isaac. She was in St Ives to persuade Joss to return home. She picked up the silk wrap and ran downstairs.

The driver told her he'd been instructed to take her to Marazion, a town on the other side of Mounts Bay from Penzance. The name was familiar because she'd seen pictures of the beach, and the little causeway linking it with a tiny island known as St Michael's Mount.

She wished she didn't feel so excited. If Gil really was here in Cornwall with Victoria, then she was about to make a complete fool of herself. But she had to know! A handsome man had smiled at her, bought her lunch in a fancy London restaurant, and apparently enjoyed her company — or had that all been part of the plan?

By the time the taxi turned into Marazion, Jenna had convinced herself that there was an ulterior motive for everything Gil Ryder did. Well, if he thought he could manipulate her, then he'd forgotten she was a Maitland!

He'd been watching for her arrival, and came forward smiling as the taxi pulled up outside the restaurant. Even in jeans, and the dark T-shirt he wore under a cream linen jacket, he managed to look devastating. Jenna was glad she'd taken so much trouble with her own appearance, and didn't miss his openly appreciative glance as she walked beside him into the restaurant.

'I'm glad you could make it, Jenna.' He smiled down at her as they followed a waiter to their table.

Despite her suspicions, she couldn't stop the gasp of admiration when she saw the view from their alcove. The whole expanse of Mounts Bay was spread before them. The castle on the island was so close that she felt if she reached out she could touch it.

'I knew you'd like it,' Gil said, and pointed. 'If you look carefully, you can just make out the causeway under the water there. We should be able to walk on it when the tide goes out a bit further.'

He took his seat opposite, watching her. This is where she was supposed to gush how clever he'd been, bringing her to such a lovely place. But she said nothing. Gil's eyes made a slow perusal of her face. Jenna concentrated on not noticing. But when his gaze dropped to her mouth and lingered there, she wasn't prepared for the delicious sensations that swept through her. The feeling was so powerful that she had to fight to keep control. Her heart was racing. This was ridiculous. She mustn't crumble now. If he even suspected the affect he was having on her, then she would lose the upper hand. She concentrated on keeping her composure and smiled across the table. This meal was not going to be easy.

Gil recommended the chargrilled artichokes served with wild rocket as a starter, followed by seared Cornish scallops with herb-rich crème fraîche. She nodded her approval. The food was complimented by a bottle of very expensive Italian Chardonnay.

As they got to the end of their meal, Jenna could feel the agitation that had been inside her all evening rising. Now was as good a time as any to confront him. She took a deep breath. 'You haven't asked me about Joss . . . if I've found him.'

Gil's head came up sharply. His eyes were wary. 'Well, have you?'

Jenna held his stare. 'I have, as it happens. We had a good talk this morning.'

Gil lifted his glass and looked away. His voice was low as he said, 'You know, don't you?'

Outside their window the cobbled causeway to St Michael's Mount was gradually emerging from the water. The sky was tinged pink, making the castle walls glow. She had to remind herself why she was here — and it was not to be seduced by the dark, admiring eyes of the man opposite.

'What's going on, Gil?' she asked quietly.

He stared at her, his brow creasing, and Jenna struggled to cling to her resolve not to be taken in by this charismatic man. But he did look genuinely sad.

She ran a finger around the rim of her glass, not looking at him. 'What exactly are you playing at?'

'Playing at?' He frowned. 'Would you mind explaining that question?' She saw the dark eyes flash with annoyance, and wondered if she could possibly have misjudged him. But she'd started this, and it was too late now to back down. Besides, there was no other way she was going to discover what was going on — or why he had chosen to involve her.

She took a leap of faith and flung the accusation at him. 'You've been stringing me along, Gil. You should have told me about Victoria.'

His face darkened and Jenna saw his jaw tighten. She braced herself for the fury that was to come, but it didn't happen. Instead, he raised his shoulders in a gesture of helplessness.

'You're right to be annoyed,' he said, quietly. 'I should have told you. I knew Joss had brought her with him to Cornwall.'

'He didn't exactly *bring* her. Joss only gave her a lift,' Jenna corrected. 'I suppose you're here to take her home.'

He ignored the implied question. 'I'm here to talk to Joss.' His sigh was deep and heartfelt. 'Look, I hated misleading you, Jenna, but I thought if you found Joss first, then you stood a better chance of persuading him to go home. He probably wouldn't even speak to me.'

Jenna's chin lifted defiantly. 'You haven't explained how you knew that Joss had given Victoria a lift down here.'

'A friend let it slip,' he said.

Jenna raised an eyebrow. 'Would this friend happen to be a Guy somebody?'

Gil stared at her. 'That's right: Guy

Bradford. But how did you know?'

'Because the same man thought Francine 'ought to know' that Joss had left Yorkshire in the company of another woman. He suggested they'd run off together.'

Gil's eyes narrowed and Jenna saw the anger flare in them.

'I can see there will be scores to settle when I get back to Yorkshire.' His voice was icy cold.

It had been on the tip of her tongue to ask what his girlfriend was doing running off to Cornwall in the first place. But then, if she was leaving him, it was none of Jenna's business. A tiny spark of hope leapt inside her when she considered the idea that Gil and Victoria might not be a happy couple after all. But it immediately fizzled out when she reminded herself that if he hadn't come here for Victoria, then he would have denied it. No, that was the real reason Gil was in Cornwall, and he'd only latched onto her because Joss was the clue to finding her.

As though he had read her thoughts, Gil spread his hands and studied them. He said, 'You're right. I do owe you an explanation. With Isaac's health the way it is, we need Joss back in Yorkshire. It might sound tough, but he has responsibilities and he needs to go back to face them.'

'And you didn't think of confiding in me?' Jenna's tone was hurt.

He held up his hands. 'OK, I was wrong,' he said. 'I should have trusted you. I just thought that, since you are so close to both Joss and Francine, that you would stand a better chance of getting through to him.'

'And what about Victoria?' Jenna's voice faltered. 'Are you seriously expecting me to believe that you didn't come to Cornwall to take her home?'

He stared at her from under a furrowed brow. 'Why would I want to do that? She's already caused enough trouble in my life.'

Jenna's eyes rounded into saucers. 'You mean she's not your girlfriend?'

Her voice had come out in a funny squeak.

'My *girlfriend*?' He looked so shocked that Jenna wanted to giggle. 'Of course she's not my girlfriend. Her parents are friends of Molly and Isaac. I took her out a couple of times, more out of courtesy to them than from any interest in her. Whatever gave you the idea that Victoria was my girlfriend?'

Somewhere inside Jenna's head, bells were ringing. She waited for him to go on, but he turned away, signalling for the bill. Neither of them spoke until the card transaction had been completed.

He was still watching her, and the connection she'd felt that first time they'd met was surging through her body again. They sat for a moment, still not speaking, and then Gil suddenly scraped back his chair and jumped to his feet, reaching for her hand.

'Come and see why I brought you here,' he said, leading her through the restaurant and out a back door where steps led down to the beach. He made no move to drop her fingers and, for a blissful few minutes, they strolled hand in hand across the sand, watching the sun sinking over Penzance. Jenna was so enchanted by the spectacular sky she hadn't noticed the evening had become chilly. She gave an involuntary shiver and Gil took off his jacket and put it round her shoulders. His hand brushed her arm and, just for a second, rested there. Jenna felt ridiculously happy. The castle's tiny windows were glinting in the reflected crimson light of the setting sun. They found a large flat stone and sat down on it.

Gil said, 'How is Joss?'

Jenna shrugged. The sky was changing by the second; mauves, pinks and peaches merging into one as the sun disappeared across the bay.

'He's alright, I suppose. He's horrified that Francine was led to believe he'd run off with another woman.'

'Does that mean he's going home?'

'I'm still working on that. I'm going to see him again tomorrow.' She smiled.

'Have you seen any of his paintings?'

'Yes. He didn't exactly show them to me. I kind of walked in on him one day while he was working on a canvas. I'm no expert, but it looked quite professional to me.'

'That's an understatement. He's actually rather a talented artist. I've asked Dad to give him an exhibition at the gallery. He says he'll think about it.'

Gil spun round to gaze at her. 'What an amazing woman you are, Jenna Maitland.' His voice was soft and his face was in shadow, but she could sense the admiration in his eyes, and a wave of tenderness swept over her. He was winning her round again, and she was more than happy to allow it to happen.

He turned, taking her face in his hands, forcing her to look into his eyes. 'It's important that you believe me, Jenna. There is absolutely nothing between Victoria and me.'

'Does she know that?' A breeze stirred the night air, and Jenna shivered as she spoke.

'You're cold,' Gil said, slipping an arm round her shoulders. She felt the warmth of his body, and a tingle ran up her spine. If what he was telling her was true, then she had totally misjudged him.

'Victoria is a wild, conniving woman,' he said. 'Never underestimate her.'

Jenna pulled his jacket closer. 'You can't choose who you fall in love with, Gil,' she said, quietly.

He ignored her words, or perhaps he hadn't heard. His voice was still angry. 'It was the money that attracted her. She liked the idea of being connected to your family's business empire. Believe me, Jenna, I've had a lucky escape.'

His eyes had been on her, and she looked up, feeling self-conscious under his gaze. He reached for her hand. 'You're a good listener, Jenna. But you should have stopped me. This was supposed to be a happy evening, and now I've spoiled it.'

Things weren't going at all as Jenna had expected. She'd been prepared to give him a chance to explain why he hadn't mentioned he was in a relationship with someone else. But she'd got the whole thing completely wrong. There had been no deception. Her heart was singing when she looked into his eyes. She sighed. 'Well, you don't do things by halves, Gil, that's for sure. But I think I'm beginning to understand you.'

'Does that mean I'm forgiven?' he asked, regarding her in such an intense way that she felt her knees go weak again.

She nodded and he took her hand, lifting her fingers to his lips. She caressed his cheek, and his eyes were moist as his mouth came down on hers. For a long, breathless moment they clung together, then his kisses strayed to her neck. Jenna could feel herself being swept away on a tide of longing. How could she ever have doubted this man?

When at last he drew back, his eyes still caressing her face in the darkness, she gazed at him breathlessly. Neither of them spoke, for the spell was too precious to break. And then he put her head on his shoulder, and they stayed like that until the final streaks of daylight had faded from the sky.

8

Jenna's emotions were in turmoil as they drove back to St Ives. She wondered if Gil was feeling the same. But every time she stole a glance at his dark profile, his face looked composed. Had he already forgotten that long, yearning kiss on the beach?

Lights strung along the seafront glinted on the water as they neared the Harbour Inn. Out in the bay, she could see the bobbing lights of anchored boats. She dared not look at Gil. But, after he pulled up outside the pub, he turned and took her in his arms. His kiss was gentle, his lips brushing her hair, her cheek, her mouth.

'Tonight's been very special, Jenna,' he murmured in her ear. 'I know you felt it too.'

Jenna reached up, her fingers exploring his face. She wanted to kiss him again ... and again. 'Tonight was special for me, too, Gil,' she whispered. 'I can't tell you how much.'

They got out of the car and strolled, hand in hand, to the harbour wall. The night air was warm and overhead was a canopy of stars. 'They look so close that I feel I could almost touch them,' she said, her head on his shoulder.

'They've come out especially for us,' Gil said quietly. 'I arranged it.'

Jenna looked into his eyes, and the tenderness she saw there took her breath away.

'I didn't know you had such power over the universe.'

'I have tonight,' he said, and his voice was husky as he bent to kiss her.

Arms entwined, they strolled slowly back to the car. 'I'll ring you,' Gil called quietly after her as she went into the pub. She turned to give him a final wave.

Upstairs in her room she lay on the bed, hugging herself. Gil had kissed her, told her the night had been special.

She'd never been so happy. His kisses were real, and the connection she'd felt between them from that very first day was real, too; she hadn't imagined it. She got up and wandered to the window, staring dreamily at the great black mass of the sea. It was then that she realized that she still had no idea where Gil was now. She knew he was staying in Cornwall, possibly somewhere nearby. But he'd never mentioned where. Why was that? she wondered sleepily.

Too tired and emotionally drained to think any more about it that night, Jenna undressed and climbed into bed. The distant sound of the waves was soothing, and she was soon asleep and dreaming of a fairytale castle high on a rock. She was climbing and Victoria was by her side, laughing as her glorious blonde hair streamed out behind. Gil was high above them, smiling at her, holding out his hand, urging her on. But when she reached him, it was Victoria's hand that he grasped, leaving Jenna to tumble down to the sea far below.

She woke with a start, her brow beaded with sweat. It was light, and she stared, frowning, around the unfamiliar room. She was still half-asleep, still climbing those rocks and gazing up into Gil's smiling face as he reached for Victoria. She shivered, but then the memories of the previous night began to swirl around her mind. That kiss had been no dream.

She was feeling happy as she climbed out of bed and went to draw back the curtains. Someone was sitting on the wall opposite, an easel in front of him, apparently painting the pub. Jenna blinked. Was she seeing right? But there was no mistaking the sun-bleached hair; the muscular, tanned body; or those awful frayed denim shorts. Joss waved across when he saw her, and she raised a hand in return. She grabbed her robe and struggled into it before opening the window.

'What are you doing here, Joss?' she called down.

'Why don't you come down and see?' he called back.

Jenna could feel the sun's warmth on her arm, and knew it was going to be another hot day. Snatching up a towel, she took the fastest shower ever, and pulled the most summery clothes she could find from the wardrobe, which happened to be her new white calf-length jeans and a lemon-and-white-striped top. The sea air and the hot Cornish sun were turning her skin more golden by the day, so the merest slick of peachy lipstick was all the make-up she needed before brushing her hair and hurrying downstairs.

Joss stood up and gave a funny little bow as she approached. 'Good afternoon, madam,' he grinned, squinting up at the sun. 'We've missed the best part of the day, but maybe there's just a little left.'

'We?' she asked, coming to stand beside him to look at his painting.

'That's right.' He nodded. 'It would be a shame to waste such a lovely day . . . ' His eyes twinkled with mischief. ' . . . even if you did look a bit dishevelled up there in your nightie.'

Jenna took a swipe at him, but she was laughing. She wandered round behind him to study the picture he'd been painting. He'd caught the essence of the old Harbour Inn perfectly: the low door where smugglers of old would have tramped through for their flagons of ale, the old sign creaking on its hinges. He'd even lightly sketched her in as she waved down to him from the window.

'It's for you,' he said. 'A present from Cornwall.'

She raised an eyebrow, wondering if this meant he had decided to go back to Yorkshire. Maybe now wasn't the time to bring it up again? But the picture was a nice thought, and she thanked him.

After he'd folded down his easel, she walked with him, stopping when they reached a dusty vehicle parked by the harbour. 'My wheels,' he said proudly, extending his hand to the dubious-looking old Jeep.

Jenna stared at it and her mouth fell open. 'You didn't seriously drive this thing all the way from Yorkshire?' She was thinking of the shiny red MG still parked in the garage at Fenfleet.

'I bought it specially, and it's perfectly adequate . . . kind of fits the image, don't you think?' he said, screwing his eyes up against the sun. 'And I've got a picnic in the back, if you're interested.'

'You're inviting me to a picnic?'

'That's about it.' He grinned. 'Think of it as an apology for yesterday. I should have been more gracious, especially since you've come all this way to see me . . . Well, I want to explain.'

Jenna pursed her lips and scrambled into the Jeep, and then they took off, roaring up the winding hill out of the town. It wasn't nearly as uncomfortable as she had imagined. Joss took the same country road as Gil had last night, but this time turned towards Penzance and followed the coast, past Newlyn fish market, where the air was pungent with the smell of the fresh landings.

Joss noticed her nose wrinkling, and threw his head back, laughing. 'Wonderful, isn't it? Newlyn's one of the biggest fishing ports in the UK now, and Cornwall is very proud of it.'

Jenna's eyes roamed over the scores of vessels bobbing at moorings in the picturesque harbour, and understood why.

'Where exactly are we going, Joss?'

'Think of it as a magical mystery tour.' He threw her a mischievous glance. 'Don't worry, you'll love it.'

Jenna's face lit up as they drove past the pretty whitewashed cottages of Mousehole, and laughed at the Jeep's reluctance to splutter up the steep climb out of the village. Soon they were back on the open road, with the hedges flying past at an alarming speed.

'This is it,' he called suddenly, pulling into a lay-by, apparently in the middle of nowhere.

Jenna looked around, puzzled; all she could see were fields. But Joss nodded ahead to a stone stile at the back of the clearing. 'There they are,' he said, pointing. 'The Merry Maidens.'

'The what?' Jenna squinted, peering through a gap in the hedge to see the ring of standing stones.

'I love painting these ancient sites, and I'm spoiled for choice in this area. Legend has it that the Maidens were a group of local girls turned to stone for dancing on the Sabbath.'

'A bit drastic, wasn't it?'

'Makes perfect sense to me,' he said, gripping Jenna's waist as she hopped off the high stone step onto the soft turf on the other side. Just for a second, she could picture Gil helping her down like this, and she looked away. She couldn't stop thinking about him.

But, just for the moment, she must put those thoughts away, and trail after Joss as he walked around the circumference of the ring. Neither of them spoke, reluctant to intrude on the spiritual feel of the place. When they'd completed the circle, Joss raised his arm and pointed ahead. 'The sea's just out there,' he said, spinning round to take in the whole site. 'I've never known such a peaceful place.'

Watching him, Jenna's mouth curved into a slow grin. He looked so like Isaac. Why hadn't she seen that before?

'Joss Maitland, you're just an old romantic.'

He turned and gave her one of his dazzling smiles. 'We artists are all romantics at heart. I thought you would have known that, Jenna.'

An artist. Jenna savoured the word. From what she'd seen of his work, he was certainly entitled to call himself that. But she wondered what Molly and Isaac would think about it. She loved Joss like a brother, but his parents always had tended to spoil him. His good looks and cavalier ways meant he was constantly the centre of attention in the well-heeled social circles of Yorkshire.

Networking was an essential part of the business world, and although the wining, dining and social side of things that was so necessary to the success of the London gallery came easily to Jenna, she had always suspected Joss was not so comfortable with it. So she'd not been surprised, on her last visit to the Maitlands' York department store, to find Joss by the window in the boardroom, quietly sketching the street scene below. When he'd heard Jenna approach he'd quickly tucked his sketchpad into his briefcase, but not before the pages flicked open, revealing other images of the city's quaint timber buildings.

The nudge on her shoulder brought her back to the present. 'Come on,' Joss was saying, heading back to the Jeep. 'We've got a picnic to eat, and I know just the place.'

They parked on the grassy top of a cliff and made their way down a steep, winding path to a cove where the sea creamed onto a white sandy beach. Jenna gasped at its beauty.

'I found this place last week,' said

Joss, dumping the heavy picnic basket on the sand. 'Isn't it great?'

Jenna's eyes scanned the horizon and fixed on the white sails of a passing yacht. 'It's beautiful,' she said, shaking out and spreading a blanket while Joss unpacked his hamper. No wonder it had been heavy; he'd tucked ice packs into every available corner to keep the food, and a bottle of wine, cool in the hot car.

'You've thought of everything,' she said, nibbling on a chicken drumstick and remembering she had missed breakfast. There were cartons of rollmop herrings, potato salad, and a quiche which he deftly cut into slices and offered to her.

'Where did you get all this stuff?' Jenna marvelled, picking up the bottle of wine.

'St Ives came out of the Dark Ages years ago,' he teased. 'And the wine's low-alcohol. Is that OK?'

Jenna sipped it and pronounced it delicious. When they'd eaten and drunk their fill, she lay back on the rug, gazing at the cloudless blue sky. A seabird circled lazily above, waiting for its chance to fly down and snatch a meal. Gil had said he would call, but so far he hadn't. She reached for her bag to check her mobile. It wasn't there. She sighed. She must have left it in her room. If he'd been ringing and got no answer, he'd think she'd been avoiding him.

'Problem?' Joss asked, looking down at her worried face.

She frowned. 'I've left my phone behind, and I was expecting a call.'

'I used to leave mine behind on purpose,' Joss said with a sigh. 'Look, Jenna. I can't put it off any longer. I'm not going back to Yorkshire, at least not yet.'

Her heart sank. 'Why not?'

He sucked in his breath and looked out across the sea. 'Call it a mid-life crisis.'

'You're not old enough to have a mid-life crisis.'

He laughed, and she saw a flash of the old Joss.

'Does Francine know this? Have you spoken to her?'

He nodded. 'And I'm very grateful to you, Jenna. Both of us are. If you hadn't come down here, we might never have sorted this out . . . well, not for a long time, and then it might have been too late.'

'You're talking in riddles, Joss. You've lost me.'

'I rang Francine after you left yesterday. I couldn't believe she thought I had gone off with another woman. Well, she knows now that that wasn't true.' He scowled and his blue eyes flashed anger. 'I'll be seeing Guy Bradford about that when I do go back to Yorkshire.'

Jenna's eyes widened. 'So you *are* going home then?'

Joss sighed, squinting at her. 'Francine and I have had a long talk. She knows I have to sort myself out. If I go home now, then Dad will think I am back for good. He'll be expecting me to take up where I left off. I don't think I can do that.' He rubbed his eyes and looked so weary that Jenna's heart reached out to him. 'I'm not cut out to run a business. If it was left to me, I'd have it in ruins in no time.'

Jenna didn't believe that for a second. She chewed her lip, thinking. 'What about Gil Ryder?' she suggested, and her heart began to flutter at the mention of his name. 'He seems to know what he's doing. Surely he would help you?'

'Gil's great, but he's not family. Besides, he's had his own problems lately. I told you about Victoria, didn't I? She's the girl I gave a lift to. She's totally besotted with him . . . won't leave him alone. That's partly why I agreed to bring her to Cornwall — to give Gil a bit of a breather. She was forever coming to Fenfleet when she knew he was there. She's determined to get him one way or another.'

Jenna froze. This wasn't what she wanted to hear. Gil had talked about his lucky escape from Victoria. Yet the woman was scheming to get him back. How far would she go? Joss's voice came from a distance.

'Francine and I have arranged to speak to each other every day,' he said. 'She texted me some pictures of the twins this morning. I might even be able to speak to them later.' He smiled and took Jenna's hand. 'The thing is . . . Francine understands why I had to come away.' His eyes were shining. 'Of course, it still doesn't make any difference to how I feel about running the family business, but at least I have an ally now, and we can make decisions together.'

The sun was high and glinting on the sea, and Joss squinted into the glare. 'I wouldn't actually have minded staying on in Yorkshire, so long as I could still paint, but that's not what my parents wanted,' he said.

'Don't you miss your family, Joss? I thought you loved your life at Fenfleet, and I'd no idea you felt like this about playing your part in the business.'

'Of course I miss the family. I miss lots of things, but the executive lifestyle . . . the suits . . . the flash cars . . . telling people what to do . . . that's not for me anymore. From the moment I opened my first box of paints on my fifth birthday, I knew I wanted to be an artist.' He sighed, narrowing his eyes again at the sun. 'My parents saw it as a hobby, an indulgence; certainly not a real job.'

He turned to her. 'I'm sure this is all very boring for you, Jenna. I hadn't planned to spend the day talking about myself.'

But Jenna shook her head. 'No, please go on.'

'St Ives is special. Being almost completely surrounded by sea, it has this wonderful clear blue light that artists love. That's why I need to be here.' They had wandered down to the water's edge, and Joss picked up a pebble and winged it into the sea.

Jenna said, 'Did you know Gil drove me down?'

Joss's eyes widened. 'You mean Gil's here in Cornwall?'

'That's right. We've all been worried about you.' She bit her lip. 'There's another thing you should know. Victoria is still here. I met her yesterday. She warned me off, said Gil was here to take her back to Yorkshire.'

Joss released a long breath. 'The little minx. What's she up to?'

Jenna shrugged. 'I don't know, but when you told me she was Gil's girlfriend . . . '

'Did I say that? What I should have mentioned is that it's all in her head. I wonder where she's staying?'

The question had also crossed Jenna's mind.

Joss was subdued as they drove back to St Ives, but as the Jeep crested the top of the town and negotiated the narrow streets, he said, 'You think I'm selfish staying down here, don't you, Jenna?'

She shook her head. 'I know you have your reasons.'

He cleared his throat before going

on. 'I know I've only been here a week or two, but I've met a few people — other artists — already. In fact, I've an invitation to an exhibition in a local gallery — and I've been asked to bring you along.'

Jenna stared at him. 'But no-one here knows me.'

He grinned, more relaxed now. 'That's where you're wrong. How long do you think it takes for word to get round a community like this that a young woman from a London gallery is in town?' He turned to see her reaction, and when she gave him a blank stare, he went on, 'They think you're some kind of talent spotter, on the hunt for new artists to make famous up in London.'

Jenna almost choked. 'They think what . . . ?'

'Well, the point is that we — both of us — have been invited to this viewing tonight. Will you come?'

'I can't wait,' she said, laughing.

9

'Jenna! I've been calling you all day! I've been worried sick. Where on earth have you been?'

She had raced to snatch up her ringing mobile as she rushed into her room. Her heart was racing when she recognized the name she was hoping to see flashing on the caller ID. 'Gil! Sorry,' she said breathlessly. 'I've been out. I left my phone behind by mistake.' She waited, heart pounding, to hear why he'd been ringing.

'I thought, perhaps you would like to go out for a meal again,' he went on hesitantly.

For an instant, Jenna thought of calling Joss, making some excuse, telling him she couldn't make it this evening after all. But she knew she couldn't do that. As much as she longed to see Gil again, she couldn't have him thinking he only had to crook a little finger for her to go running to him. She'd made a promise to Joss and she would keep it. But she was in no doubt as to who she would rather be spending the evening with.

'My loss is Joss's gain, then.' Gil gave a disappointed sigh. She could hear the regret in his voice, and her heart turned over. 'How is Joss, anyway?' he asked. 'Have you persuaded him to go home yet?'

'I'm getting there. I think he just needs a bit of time. But he's fine. In fact, he's starting to make new friends down here. This artist whose work we're going to see tonight is one of them.'

'That doesn't sound like he's considering going home.'

'Like I said, give him time.'

'If you say so. I'm sure you know what you're doing. Just don't buy too many of those paintings tonight, will you?' He was making an effort to sound light-hearted, but Jenna hadn't been fooled. He'd wanted to see her, and she had let him down. Gil cleared his throat. 'I miss you, Jenna.' His voice was husky. 'I'll ring in the morning.'

She sat staring at the phone for a long time after he'd rung off. Gil was missing her! His words rang in her head. She longed to call him back, say she'd changed her mind. But instead, she showered and changed and went downstairs to wait for Joss. She was nursing a glass of red wine in the bar when her cousin walked in and relieved her of it.

'There will be plenty of this at the viewing,' he said, taking the glass from her hand and putting it back on the bar counter. 'Vinnie won't be stinting on the booze, not from what I've heard.'

'Vinnie? Is that our host's name?'

He nodded. 'Vincent Pemberley-Jones . . . alias the mentor to Cornwall's idle rich . . . and as much of a poser as his name suggests.'

'If you don't like him, then why are we going to his exhibition?'

'I didn't say I didn't like him,' Joss said, propelling her out of the bar into the warm evening sunshine. 'His work isn't bad, but it isn't everybody's idea of art. However, there's no harm in checking out what the opposition is doing.'

Vincent Pemberley-Jones's gallery was half-way along the seafront. Its retro-style black-and-white facade gave it the appearance of a trendy wine bar, but no one could miss the excessively dominant lettering of *The Gallery* above the large plate-glass window. Jenna remembered stopping at the place and glancing in while she was exploring St Ives. It had been closed then, but the colourful paintings inside were intriguing, and she was looking forward to seeing them properly.

They were early, but the party was already in full swing. Jenna thought she recognized a few London faces amongst the expensively-dressed guests. A tall, willowy blonde, in a long tartan skirt and white silk blouse, appeared bearing a tray of champagne flutes which she offered to the new arrivals. They each accepted one and began to mingle. Joss spotted someone he recognized and went off to greet him. Jenna took her chance to wander round the exhibition, studying each of the over-sized canvases in turn. They were not to her taste, but Joss was right: they weren't bad. And the interior designers loved this colourful stuff, with its great streaks of aquamarine and blue sandwiched between swatches of yellows, pinks and peaches. The artist obviously saw himself as working in the contemporary field. She thought of Joss's painting of Victoria, how he'd captured that moment of abandon as her green eyes flashed defiance. It had been full of passion — exactly what the paintings in front of her lacked. But if Mr Pemberley-Jones enjoyed what he was doing, then who was she to say otherwise?

She hadn't noticed Joss come up behind her, and started when he hissed in her ear, 'What d'you think?'

They were standing before a floor-to-ceiling composition comprising blocks of colour where the paints had been allowed to drip into each other.

Jenna raised an eyebrow. 'Well, it's different.'

'Different enough to meet with your approval?' a voice from over her shoulder asked.

She wheeled round and found herself staring into the amused face of a tall, wiry man a little older than herself. His mass of wavy brown hair fell to his shoulders, and his sharply-chiselled features gave him a superior air. Jenna recognized the rakish challenge in the teasing grey eyes.

He offered his hand. 'Vincent Pemberley-Jones, at your service.' He made a show of clicking his heels together, but the sandals he wore rendered the gesture pointless, and made him look a little ridiculous. 'But you can call me Vinnie, everyone else does.' Still holding Jenna's hand, he moved forward, placing himself between her and Joss. 'And you are . . . ?

Jenna was in no doubt that he already

knew perfectly well who she was, but she inclined her head and introduced herself anyway.

He waved a hand around the exhibits before turning to study her again. 'So, Jenna, what do you think of my work?'

Frantically, she searched for a description that would cause no offence. 'It has impact,' she said, smiling. Joss looked away and she knew that he was hiding a grin.

Taking a firm grip of her shoulders, Vinnie turned her round and began propelling her through the gallery. 'You must see my studio,' he said.

She flashed a look that screamed 'rescue me' at Joss, and he was by her side in an instant. 'Great idea, Vinnie,' he said, slapping the other man's back. 'I'd love to see where you work. Lead on.'

For a second, Vinnie fixed Joss with a contemptuous glare, but he could hardly start a scene in his own packed gallery, so he led them upstairs to his flat and into a room that streamed with light. Paints and canvases were every-where. A colour-encrusted tarpaulin on the floor made Jenna wonder if he abandoned his palette and brushes in favour of a can of spray paint.

'Well,' he said, waving his hand around the room in a gesture of pride, 'this is where it all happens.'

Jenna sneaked a glance at Joss, who was trying to disguise his astonishment. 'I'm speechless,' she said.

Vinnie took this to be a compliment, and pulled out more canvases for further praise.

'Actually, could I just use your loo before I study your work in detail?' Jenna cut in.

Vinnie looked surprised, but nodded and pointed her along the landing. Leaving Joss to the full force of Vinnie's descriptions of how he worked, Jenna made her way along the landing, passing a door that was slightly open. Inside, she could see more paintings lining the walls; assuming this to be another, smaller gallery, she stepped inside. Too late, she realized she was in Vinnie's bedroom. As she turned to leave, a picture hanging above the bed stopped her in her tracks. It was Victoria! But not the wholesome wind-blown girl in Joss's painting. This Victoria was posing provocatively over a chaise longue, a flimsy white wrap not quite covering her nakedness. This was the woman Gil had taken out. Jenna felt her throat go dry as she stared at the painting.

She hadn't heard the other door open, so the woman's voice behind her took her by surprise. 'Seen enough?' it said.

Jenna turned, caught like a guilty child with her fingers in the honey jar. He cheeks flamed as she came face to face with the woman in the painting. Victoria's cat eyes narrowed and flashed with menace as she advanced on Jenna. She pushed her face close, as she had done on their last encounter. 'Snooping, are we?' Her words were sneering, but there was a glint of triumph there.

Jenna used the split second to regain her composure. 'You do get around, Victoria. But why are you hiding away up here? I thought you would have been flaunting yourself downstairs this evening.'

A shadow of annoyance crossed the lovely face, before Victoria's chin lifted. 'I don't mix with that lot. I prefer more entertaining company. Besides . . . ' Her eyes glinted with triumph. ' . . . Vinnie prefers to have me all to himself.'

'I didn't realize you two were such good friends.'

Victoria's eyes sparkled. 'More than friends. He wants me to marry him . . . has done for years.'

'What's stopping you, then?

'I have other plans,' she said, and then hesitated before adding, 'So what does Gil's latest . . . ' The corner of her mouth rose in a sneer. ' . . . well, what would you call yourself?' she mocked.

Jenna heaved a sigh. The woman was becoming tiresome. She matched Victoria's defiant stare. 'I'd call us friends,' she said. 'And I'd still like to know what business it is of yours.'

Victoria pouted. 'He's told you about us, hasn't he?' She inclined her head even closer to Jenna's face. 'Has he also told you that he still loves me and would do anything to get me back?'

Jenna froze. Even though she was certain the girl was lying, the suggestion sent warning bells clanging in her head. She took a steadying breath. 'Strangely enough, no.' There was more she could have added, but she didn't want to engage with Victoria Symington any more than she had to.

'I've seen you two together . . . kissing when he drops you off at the pub. He's playing games with you . . . you'll see.' The words were laced with venom.

Jenna bit her lip, determined not to rise to this bait. She turned to go, but Victoria caught her arm. She was smiling. 'I'll be watching you, just remember that.'

Jenna pulled her arm free and held her head high as she walked away, but inside she was shaking. She was in no doubt that Victoria was capable of causing trouble.

Along the landing she could hear Joss and Vinnie still talking in the studio, but her mind was racing, trying to make sense of what had just happened.

She was thoughtful, distracted, as they left Vinnie's gallery an hour later.

'Like to come back for a coffee?' Joss offered.

'Actually,' Jenna said, 'would you mind if I just go back to my room? I was fancying an early night.' She needed time to think. 'But I do want to see you tomorrow, Joss. Maybe I could come along in the morning?'

Joss shrugged. 'Why not? But come early, I've got work planned.'

Jenna watched him head off towards Seagull Cottage, and wondered why she hadn't told him about Victoria. Maybe she should have? She was back in her room before the thought struck her. She'd been so shocked at being confronted by the girl that she hadn't wondered until now what she'd been doing at Vinnie's place. She'd been wearing jeans and light sandals, and had looked completely at home there.

Jenna sat bolt upright on the bed. That was it. Victoria was living with Vinnie! It was obvious now. She wondered if she should warn Gil.

A bright sun woke Jenna early next morning, and the waitress in the Harbour Inn's dining room raised a surprised eyebrow at the sight of her sauntering in at seven-thirty.

'You're first down,' she said. 'I think some of the old St Ives magic is beginning to rub off on you.'

'You could be right,' Jenna laughed.

Half an hour later, after a breakfast of delicious smoked haddock and hot buttered toast, she was outside with the smell of the sea in her nostrils. This time, she'd made sure her phone was safely in her pocket. She didn't want to risk missing Gil's call. On an impulse, she kicked off her sandals and ran down the slipway in front of the pub to the beach. Her toes curled into the warm sand and she raised her face to the sun. In the distance, she could see the harbour already buzzing with activity.

It was just before nine when she climbed the stairs to Joss's cottage.

'Just in time for coffee,' he grinned.

This time his jeans were clean and he was wearing a fresh T-shirt. Going by the faint smell of soap, he had already showered. This was more like the Joss she knew. He pointed through to the sitting room.

'I'd prefer to go through to the studio, if that's alright with you,' she said, already heading in that direction.

'It's fine. Make yourself at home,' Joss called from the kitchen.

The sliding glass doors to the veranda had been thrown open and the pungent, salty smells of the harbour filled the room. The first thing she spotted was the painting of herself at the window of the Harbour Inn. It was on the easel and he'd been working on it. To Jenna's eye it looked finished.

'You must take it back with you,' Joss

said, appearing with two steaming mugs of coffee.

'I love it. Thank you, Joss.'

'My pleasure.'

He settled himself on a three-legged stool in the corner, indicating Jenna should take the more comfortable chair by the window.

'I spoke to my folks last evening.'

She nodded. 'How were they?'

'Happy to know I'm safe and well.' He frowned. 'Dad sounded a little tired.'

'They're missing their son, Joss.'

He put his mug on the stone floor. 'I've said I'd call them again today, after I've spoken to Francine again.'

'That's great, Joss. All they've ever asked is that you keep in touch.'

'Not quite all,' Joss said. 'They still want me to go home. I'm still not ready to do that.'

Jenna got up and crossed to the painting on the easel. 'This is really good. You've got a knack.'

He laughed, inclining his head at the

compliment. 'You see,' he said, 'I don't always paint dark subjects.'

'I met Victoria again last night, Joss . . . at Vinnie's. I think she's living with him.'

'Well . . . the little madam! So that's where she's been.' He shook his head. 'And what a dark horse that Vinnie is. But if it gets her off Gil Ryder's back, then maybe it's no bad thing.'

Jenna took a deep breath. 'She says Gil wants her back.'

Joss laughed. 'In her dreams. Victoria made his life a nightmare. Oh, I know she's gorgeous-looking and everything, but the best thing Gil ever did was steer clear of her.'

Jenna's heart was beginning to soar. How could she have doubted Gil?

She was in high spirits as she set off back to the Harbour Inn. Gil still hadn't phoned, but she was sure now that he would. She'd been on an emotional rollercoaster ever since he walked into her dad's London gallery. Even now, her head was full of pictures. There was the bistro in Covent Garden, when Gil had gazed at her so intently that her knees had turned to jelly, and the day in Polperro when he'd given her the lucky Cornish charm — and then that kiss on the beach at Marazion, when they were almost swept away by their passion for each other. Had that only been two nights ago?

She'd reached the corner of Joss's road when she saw him. Her heart began to hammer. 'Gil!' she called, trying to keep her voice steady. 'What are you doing here?'

His eyes slid towards Joss's cottage. 'I'm taking a leaf out of your book and having one last attempt at persuading Joss to go home.'

The alarm bells rang. She reached out to touch his arm. 'Last attempt? That sounds quite final, Gil.'

He smiled back, but his eyes were serious. 'I'm going back to Yorkshire,' he said. 'You can stay on, of course. Just let me know when you're ready to leave, and I'll book you a flight from Newquay.'

The sun had slipped behind a cloud and Jenna's heart went with it. She hadn't been expecting this.

'The work's piling up there, and I don't want to leave it all to Isaac. I have to get back to attend to things.'

Jenna nodded, determined not to look as miserable as she now felt. 'I'm sure Isaac will appreciate that.' Her voice sounded strangely weak. She thrust out her hand. 'Well, goodbye, Gil,' she said, not daring to look at him.

But he didn't take her hand, and when she glanced up he was studying her with a look that made her tingle.

'It's not goodbye . . . not yet, I hope. Can I catch up with you in — ' He checked his watch. ' — say, about half an hour?'

Jenna had to fight to find her voice. In the end, she just nodded.

'Great. I'll see you back at the Harbour Inn, then.' His wide, sensitive mouth took on a grim line and his brow furrowed. 'Wish me luck,' he said.

'I do,' she called after him as he

turned back towards Joss's cottage.

The first tears began to blur her vision as she reached the seafront. She was attracting curious looks as she desperately tried to blink them away. All she could think of was that Gil was leaving Cornwall.

When she arrived at the inn, she didn't go inside, but crossed instead to the beach and sat on the low wall. A young couple was struggling to launch a dinghy from a trailer, laughing across at each other as they eventually managed to free the little boat and drag it down to the water. They looked so happy. Jenna bit her lip and kept her eye on the road. The last thing she wanted was to miss Gil when he came back.

Less than twenty minutes later, she spotted his dark head and the sleeveless denim shirt he had been wearing. She frowned. He hadn't been long. Did this mean his meeting with Joss hadn't gone well? She got up and strolled to meet him. He was smiling, and this time the smile reached his eyes.

'Well, it's wasn't exactly happy families back there, but at least he heard me out. So I suppose that's progress,' he said.

'It sounds hopeful enough to me,' Jenna said, forcing back the lump in her throat. 'I suppose you'll be off back to Yorkshire now?'

'Not till this evening,' he said lightly. 'I was hoping we could spend some time together before then.'

He nodded across to the boats tied up by the harbour wall. 'How good a sailor are you?'

Jenna stared at him.

'I know a little cove just along the coast where we can swim.'

'I don't have a costume,' she laughed.

'Never mind. You can sunbathe instead — and feel very jealous, of course, watching me swim.'

'Are you serious?'

'Never more so. Can you see that little blue-and-white motor launch?' He pointed over to the boats. 'Well that's our transport.'

He grabbed her hand, grinning, and began to stride towards the boats. 'And we're wasting time.'

'When did you arrange all this?' she demanded as she sat back, gasping, after he had helped her clamber down onto the launch. 'It's only just after ten now. You must have been up at dawn to hire this boat.'

'It's my parents' boat; I told you they had a place down here,' he shouted as the engine sprang into life, drowning his words.

Safely strapped into her lifejacket, Jenna threw her arms to the wind, laughing as they sped along the coast, passing the great white shape of the Tate St Ives. 'Dad will never believe this,' she called.

The wind was tearing at their hair, making their eyes water. The sense of freedom was exhilarating. Less than an hour ago, she'd been plunged into despair at the thought of never seeing Gil again. Now, here she was . . . right by his side as they skimmed over the waves. Their parting would come soon enough, but for now they had this whole suddenly wonderful day ahead of them — and Jenna knew it would be bliss.

'That's our cove,' Gil shouted, cutting the engine's power to coast towards the tiny curve of white sand.

She could see a beach, surrounded by steep granite cliffs, and a twisting path that threaded its way to the top. 'It's beautiful,' she gasped. 'How do you know about this place?'

But her question was answered as they glided towards the cove and headed for the wooden landing. It was evident, as they came alongside and Gil tied up the boat and steadied it for Jenna to hop off, that he was no stranger to this place.

'You're full of surprises, Gil,' she breathed, spinning round to take in the expanse of turquoise sea. 'This place is just beautiful.'

'I thought you'd approve,' he said, pulling a blanket and towels from the boat's tiny cabin.

'Here,' he laughed, tossing them at her. 'Make yourself useful.'

As Jenna spread the blanket on the warm sand, Gil disappeared behind a rock and emerged moments later in black swimming trunks.

'I've been looking forward to this all week,' he called, as he ran past her to the sea.

She laughed, lying back, propping herself onto her elbows to watch him. He was a strong swimmer, and she wished she could have joined him. She could imagine the sensation of that cold water rippling over their bodies as they struck out through the waves together. An exquisite shiver ran through her and she held up her face to the sun.

It was ten minutes before Gil emerged from the sea. Jenna held her breath as she watched him run up the beach towards her, beads of water glistening on every inch of his strong, tanned body. She picked up the towel and handed it up to him.

'You're a good swimmer,' she said, trying not to sound too impressed.

He collapsed down beside her, unselfconsciously towelling himself dry. His closeness was doing strange things to her body. She should stand up and walk away from him. Instead, she scanned the horizon, her eyes fixing on the white sails of a passing yacht.

'It's spectacular here, isn't it,' he said. 'I knew you would like it, Jenna.'

Even the sound of her name on his lips made her feel weak. She took a deep breath, forcing herself to stay calm. She lay back on the blanket, watching a seagull making lazy circles in the sky. The sun was warm on her face.

'You'll burn,' Gil said, leaning across her unexpectedly to reach for the tube of sun cream he'd brought from the boat. Jenna's heart was thudding. She stared, mesmerized, at his hands as they slowly unscrewed the cap. He touched the cream to her bare shoulders, moved it in caressing strokes down her arms.

When his mouth came down on hers, it was gentle, loving, and Jenna felt herself being swept away in a tide of longing. But it was all happening too fast. He was leaving for Yorkshire that evening, and she'd be alone again. She pushed him gently away, scrambling to her feet. She ran down to the water's edge, her feelings in turmoil. She had wanted Gil to kiss her, but now he was leaving . . .

He came after her. 'I'm sorry, Jenna,' he said. 'I thought you felt the same way as I do.' He was standing so close that she could smell the salt on his skin. 'I know I haven't given you much cause to trust me. I should have told you about Victoria straight away.' His voice trailed off and he spoke so quietly that she had to strain to hear him. 'I've never felt like this before, Jenna, and I just don't know how to deal with it.'

Her breath caught in her throat as she turned to him, hardly daring to believe what she was hearing. But when she looked into his eyes, she saw such tenderness that she was powerless to stop her tears from spilling over. His fingers wiped them gently away, and he took her in his arms again.

'I think I'm falling in love with you, Jenna,' he said, his voice husky.

'I think that might be mutual, Gil,' she said, her own voice coming out in a strange croak.

It was an hour before they made a move to leave the beach. Gil grinned down at her. 'Hungry?'

'Don't tell me you've brought a picnic?' she laughed, propping herself up on one elbow.

'Nothing so grand,' he said. 'But I do know where we could find a meal.' He nodded towards the winding path.

Jenna stared at him in disbelief. 'You're not telling me there's a pub up there?'

He shook his head, gathering up the towels and blanket to put them back on the boat.

'Come and see,' he said, taking Jenna's hand and guiding her up the steep climb.

When they reached the top, her eyes

rounded and her mouth fell open. She was staring at one of the prettiest houses she had ever seen. It looked like an old farmhouse with various out-buildings, and sat in the middle of a delightful cottage garden. The building was far enough back from the cliff top to be invisible from below, but its view from up here was stunning. Borders cascaded with pink and white geraniums, and the smell of roses and honeysuckle was everywhere.

Jenna gasped. 'Who lives here?

'I do,' Gil said. 'And if we're lucky, Eva will have kept some lunch for us.'

Jenna was struggling to take all this in. 'Eva?' she asked, bemused.

Gil nodded. 'Nick and Eva look after the house. My folks bought Eagle's Crest about ten years ago.' He glanced at her, enjoying her confusion. 'I told you we had a place in Cornwall.'

'But I thought it was a cottage — '

'It's a bit bigger than that.' He grinned. 'Seven bedrooms, I think, at the last count.'

Jenna threw out her arms. 'All this, and Joss lives in that awful dilapidated cottage. Couldn't you let him stay here?'

Gil sighed. 'He might get too comfortable and never leave. I don't think Molly and Isaac would appreciate that,' he said. 'But I promised you a meal, so let's see if we can find it.'

He took Jenna's hand and led her inside the house. A plump, smiling woman bustled up to meet them. 'Mr Gil, we were beginning to think you were never coming.' She gave a brief, friendly nod to Jenna after Gil introduced them, then carried on, 'I thought it was too hot today for anything more than a salad, but there's some cold beef in the fridge, and a bit of fresh salmon to go with it. It's all waiting for you in the kitchen.'

She ushered them through, adding, 'Nick and me, we have to go into St Ives this afternoon, so we'll just leave you to get on with it.'

Gil put an arm round Eva's shoulder

and gave it a squeeze. 'Get off with you, woman. We'll manage just fine.'

Eva threw a flustered smile in Jenna's direction before hurrying out. A few minutes later, they heard a car start.

'Treasures, the pair of them,' Gil laughed. 'Even if they do boss us about most of the time.'

'They live here permanently, then?' Jenna asked, swallowing a mouthful of Eva's delicious beef.

Gil nodded. 'Mum advertised for a couple to look after the house. Basically, they just keep an eye on things. Nick keeps the gardens tidy and Eva attends to the house. They've got a tiny little cottage down at the end of the garden.'

'It's beautiful,' Jenna said, gazing round the impressive farmhouse kitchen. 'Does the little cove below also belong to the property?'

'It does.' Gil nodded. 'Dad loves going out on the boat. I think he'd get on with your dad. I can just see the pair of them out there fishing on a day like this.'

Jenna liked the idea of that, but the

mention of her father reminded her she'd soon be returning to London, and although she no longer believed that she would never see Gil again, she was going to miss him. 'When are you planning to set off for Yorkshire?' she asked, trying to keep her voice casual.

'Almost straight away, I'm afraid. When we've finished lunch, I'll drive you back to St Ives and just carry on from there. My bags are all packed and in the car.'

The thought of Gil leaving so soon was now casting a shadow over the day.

He reached across the table. 'I know,' he said, holding her gaze, 'I don't want to go . . . especially not now. But I'll ring every day.'

Jenna nodded, swallowing hard to stop the tears falling. Though she knew he couldn't stay in Cornwall indefinitely, it felt like a magical part of her life was coming to an end.

'Don't work too hard when you get back to Yorkshire,' she said when Gil dropped her off at the Harbour Inn.

This time, he made no apologies for gathering her into his arms and kissing her.

'I'll be seeing you soon,' he said, gazing into her eyes.

'Yes, Gil,' she whispered.

10

It was the middle of the night when Jenna's phone rang, waking her from a fitful sleep. Her first thought was for her father. Had something happened to him . . . or was it the gallery? Instantly awake, her hand shot out towards the blinking blue light. But it wasn't Daniel's name flashing on the tiny screen. She didn't recognize the number. She struggled up and clicked the answer button.

'Jenna! Thank God!' Joss's voice was full of panic.

'OK, Joss, calm down. Just tell me what's happened.'

'It's Dad. He's had a heart attack!'

Jenna's head was still dealing with the relief that the emergency did not involve her own father. Then the reality struck her. He was talking about Isaac! The words 'heart attack' kept flashing through her mind. Did this mean her uncle was dead? She cleared her throat, hardly daring to ask. 'How bad is it, Joss?'

His voice was shaking. 'He's very poorly. Gil and my mother are with him at the hospital.'

Jenna heard him take a deep breath. She had a brief image of Gil's arm around Molly's shoulders as he comforted her. She was fully alert now. 'Right, Joss,' she said. 'You need to get home. I'm coming with you!'

'Gil has booked us a couple of flights from Newquay, but we need to leave right away. Can you throw a few things in a bag?'

She was already scrambling out of bed and on her way to the shower. She estimated it would take Joss no more than ten minutes to get to the Harbour Inn. There was no time to waste. A minute under the hot running water was enough to revive her before she dashed round the room grabbing essential items and tossing them into her case. It was still dark when she hurried downstairs, leaving a note on the bar for Mike — explaining her sudden disappearance, and that she would be in touch later to settle up for the room.

Joss's battered Jeep was already at the side door of the pub as Jenna hurried out. She didn't miss the lines of worry etched on his face as he took her cases and tossed them into the back of the vehicle. She put her arms around him and for a second they clung together.

'Isaac will get through this, Joss,' she said. 'We'll make sure he does.'

He gave a grim nod, helping her to scramble into the vehicle.

It was barely light, but there was already movement in the harbour. Jenna could glimpse shadowy figures moving about on the quay, more activity on the boats below, as the St Ives fishermen made ready to put to sea.

Two hours later, Jenna and Joss were airborne, flying high above the Cornish coast and heading for Yorkshire. Somewhere below was the tiny cove of white sand where Gil had kissed her and told her he loved her. That magical after-noon seemed to belong to another world now.

Joss's voice cut into her thoughts. 'Gil's meeting us at the other end,' he said as their aircraft rose above the clouds.

The mention of his name caused Jenna's heart to flutter, but this time it was strangely comforting. Until now there hadn't been time to think about anything else but her Uncle Isaac. She'd tried to ring her father from the airport, but there had been no reply. In normal circumstances she would have worried about that, but these were not normal circumstances. She glanced at Joss, slumped in the seat beside her. He looked so anxious and vulnerable that she wanted to hug him. Instead, she touched his arm and gave him what she hoped was a reassuring smile.

'Are you OK, Joss?'

He nodded. He'd been miles away, probably in that hospital ward with his dad.

'Isaac is a fighter,' she said, gently. 'He *will* come through this.'

Joss gave her a weary smile. 'Dad's tough, all right; I know that. But all the difficult times he's had in the past have been to do with the business, never his health. I think this is the first time he's ever actually been seriously ill.' He shook his head. 'I should have been there.'

'Well, you soon will be. We should be landing shortly.' Jenna's heart gave a little lurch. She was already imagining Gil walking towards them when they reached the airport arrivals lounge.

The flight was short, and it seemed to Jenna that they had only just taken off when they were landing again.

They hurried through the formalities, eventually emerging in the vast passenger lounge. Gil's face lit up the second he spotted them coming towards him. Then she saw the concern in his eyes as his glance switched to Joss. He took Jenna's cases.

'The car's this way,' he said, leading

them out of the airport. He was wearing a red polo-necked sweater under a black leather jacket and looked so handsome that, even under these circumstances, Jenna's pulse quickened.

'How's Dad?' Joss asked, as they all hurried across the car park.

Gil tried to sound reassuring. 'He's holding his own. That's about as much as the hospital will tell us.'

They reached the car, and Gil swung their cases into the boot. He smiled, but he didn't fool Jenna. She could see it was strained. A frightening chill suddenly gripped at her heart. For the first time, she realized that Isaac might actually die. She began to tremble. She couldn't fall apart now. She was there to support everyone.

'And Mum? How's she coping with all this?' Joss said.

'You know Molly. She copes with everything. But she'll be really pleased to see you, Joss . . . both of them will.'

Joss nodded and glanced away, but not before Jenna noticed the wetness in his eyes. Isaac was his father. He was bound to feel all this even more than her. Trying to keep negative thoughts at bay, she wondered if her uncle's illness would change anything . . . if Joss would now give up any idea of an artist's life in Cornwall and move back here. The countryside was certainly beautiful enough, she thought, gazing out at the rolling fields and distant hills of North Yorkshire. This part of the country had a rugged coastline peppered with scenic fishing villages, not unlike those in Cornwall. Jenna thought that, if Joss moved back home, he would certainly not be short of subjects to paint here.

They threaded their way along the familiar country roads until they reached the stone pillars that flanked the entrance to Fenfleet. Gil slowed the car, its tyres crunching on the gravelled drive, as the beautiful old house came into view. Despite her years in London, this was what Jenna always thought of as home.

Molly Maitland had been waiting at the open door to greet them, and she rushed forward, arms wide open, when she caught sight of Joss. Mother and son shared an emotional hug.

'How is Dad?' Joss asked gently.

Jenna was shocked to see how frail and exhausted Molly looked. She was also fighting to hold back tears.

'We don't really know yet.' Her voice shook, and Jenna saw the damp hankie crumpled tightly into her fist. 'He was so poorly last night, Joss. I didn't want to leave him, but the doctor insisted I should come home for a rest.' She twisted the hankie. 'I should be there with him now.'

'We'll go together,' Joss said, gathering his mother into another embrace.

Only then did she notice Jenna, and come forward to embrace her. Apart from the worry lines now etched on her face, Molly was still Molly, a small, slightly plump woman, whose prettily-styled fair hair was showing the first signs of greying at the temples.

Jenna smiled. Even under circumstances such as these, standards had to be maintained. Molly had dressed smartly, in a simple pale grey linen dress, with a choker of pearls at her throat.

'Thank you, Jenna,' she said, drawing her niece close. 'I can't tell you what a comfort it is to have you here with us.'

Jenna shrugged, embarrassed. 'Please don't thank me, Molly. I haven't done anything.'

'You brought our son home,' she said, her voice no more than a shaky murmur.

Turning to Gil, she said, 'Will you be kind enough to help Jenna with her things?' Then, smiling at Jenna, she added, 'You're in the same room, dear.'

Jenna glanced back as she walked ahead of Gil up the sweeping staircase. Joss and Molly were strolling, arms entwined, in the direction of the drawing room. They had a lot of talking to do.

She had a feeling of déjà vu as she

went into the friendly bright bedroom. Gil followed her in, closing the door behind them before gathering her into his arms. When his mouth found hers, his kiss was deep and hungry. 'I can't believe you're really here,' he whispered, huskily.

But Jenna was in no state to reply; his kiss had left her breathless. She moved out of his arms to regain her composure. 'What about Isaac, Gil? How ill is he really?'

Gil sat down heavily on the bed and ran a hand through his dark hair. He shook his head. 'Not great. Molly and I have been at his bedside most of the night. She's only home now because the doctors insisted she must have some rest away from the hospital. Even then, I had to drag her away. She can't wait to get back again.'

He stood up and came over, taking her in his arms again. 'I'll go back with Molly and Joss this afternoon. If you don't mind staying here to keep Francine company, that is?'

Jenna reached up and kissed him gently on the mouth. 'I want to see Isaac as well, but Francine and I do have some catching up to do,' she said, linking arms with him as they went back downstairs.

They found Molly alone in the drawing room when they walked in. She looked up and gave them a wan smile. 'Joss is through in the bungalow with Francine and the children. They need some time on their own.' She nodded back to the drinks tray. 'Pour Jenna a sherry, would you, dear.'

Obediently, Gil headed for the collection of bottles assembled on the long table behind one of the sofas.

'Never mind the drink, Molly,' Jenna said, sitting down beside her aunt. 'Is there anything I can do to help?'

Molly gave a weak smile and patted Jenna's arm. 'You're already doing it just by being here.'

Despite her refusal, Gil handed Jenna a glass of sherry, and she nodded her thanks before turning back to Molly. 'I meant what I said. I really do want to help. You only have to say.'

'Thank you, Jenna, I appreciate that.' She stood up and turned to Gil. 'I think I'll skip lunch. I might just lie down for an hour before we go back to the hospital.'

Jenna jumped up and put an arm round the older woman's shoulders. 'Take as long as you like, Molly. But surely there's no need for you to go rushing back to the hospital.' She glanced across at Gil. 'We're all here now, so we can take it in turns to sit with Isaac.'

'Jenna's right. You need to rest, Molly,' Gil said. 'We don't want you falling ill, too.'

'You see what I have to put up with?' Molly threw a conspiratorial grin at Jenna. 'Stop fussing, Gil dear. I've said I'll be down in a hour, and I will.'

'She's completely whacked,' Gil said, when Molly had left the room. He sank down on the sofa opposite Jenna.

She could see the weariness in his

own eyes and got up to sit next to him. 'What exactly happened with Isaac?' she asked quietly. 'I want to know everything.'

Gil ran a hand over his dark hair, his eyes sombre as he relived the events of the previous night. 'I'd only just arrived back from Cornwall — I came straight to Fenfleet to tell Molly and Isaac about my meeting with Joss. I knew something was wrong with Isaac the minute I saw him. His face was grey and there were beads of sweat on his forehead. He'd been working in his study, and got up to greet me as I went in.'

Gil closed his eyes and his face contorted at the memory. He took a deep breath. 'Isaac suddenly clutched at his chest and just kind of crumpled to the floor. Molly flew across the room to him and began giving him resuscitation. She was amazing. I grabbed my phone to get an ambulance.'

Jenna nodded. She remembered the First Aid course the company had offered to all Maitland employees. She and Molly had also enlisted. She thanked God now that she had.

'The ambulance seemed to take forever to arrive, but in reality it could only have been a few minutes.' Gil's hand went through his hair again. 'The paramedics were brilliant. They took over from Molly and managed to bring him round, then it was a frantic dash to get him to the hospital in York.' He met Jenna's eyes and said quietly, 'Molly saved Isaac's life.'

They hadn't noticed Joss come into the room. But he'd heard them. 'And I wasn't even here,' he was muttering miserably. 'I should have come back with you yesterday, Gil, when you told me Dad was off-colour.'

Jenna saw Gil's brows come together in the familiar frown. 'Don't beat yourself up, Joss. None of us could have known this would happen.'

She looked from one to the other. 'I feel so helpless. Isn't there anything I can do?'

Joss gave her a grateful smile. 'There is, actually. I know you probably want to come to the hospital with us, but is there any chance you can stay here with Francine? She could do with a shoulder to lean on.'

Jenna smiled. 'Of course I will.'

They all looked up when a young woman with ginger hair and a freckled face came into the room and announced that lunch was served.

'I won't join you,' Joss said. 'I'm having something with Fran and the twins. But you two go ahead.'

After Joss had returned to join his family, Jenna followed Gil through the connecting double doors into the adjoining dining room, each taking their place at a long table that had been set for four.

'It's only something simple, sir,' the woman addressed Gil. 'Cauliflower cheese and a few slices of ham.'

'Thanks, Maria.' Gil smiled. 'That sounds perfect.'

Neither of them was particularly

hungry, but the food was tasty and they made an effort to finish most of what was placed before them. Exactly an hour after she had left them, Molly reappeared. She looked refreshed and brighter, and had changed into a powder-blue skirt and jacket. Joss and Francine followed her into the room, each grasping the hand of a twin. Jenna hadn't seen the children since before she left for Cornwall, and bent down to hug them. Charlotte, her head a mass of springy blonde curls, gave her a shy smile. But her brother, Alfie, wailed, 'Where's Grandpa . . . I want Grandpa.'

Jenna held the little face gently in her hands and used a finger to brush away a tear. 'I'm sure Daddy will tell Grandpa how much you and Charlotte are missing him.' In her peripheral vision, she saw Molly turn away, a hand at her eyes. And when she looked up at Joss, he had a lump in his throat.

'Well, if everybody's ready, I think we should get off,' Gil said.

Jenna stood with Francine and the

children, waving the three of them off as Gil's car crunched down the drive. She had her fingers firmly crossed that the news they brought back about Isaac would be good.

11

The patio doors of the bungalow were open, and the children's voices drifted in from the garden. Jenna smiled as she watched them play. 'I can't believe how much they've grown since I was last here.'

Francine was cradling a mug of coffee, but her eyes were distant. 'Is Joss home for good?' She held up a hand to silence Jenna's response. 'It's OK. You don't have to answer that. I can see from your face that he isn't.'

Jenna bit her lip, hating to see her friend in such turmoil. 'I think he's beginning to work things out,' she said. Then, leaning forward to emphasize her point: 'What I do know for sure is that he's been missing you and — ' She nodded out to the garden where Charlotte and Alfie were taking turns to hurtle down a brightly-coloured slide. ' — these two. He was a different man after he spoke to you.'

Francine shook her head, dejectedly. 'Then why won't he stay with us? I don't know what to do, Jenna, I feel so helpless.'

'Well, at least you know he didn't run off with another woman.'

Francine's shoulders heaved in a long sigh. 'I never really believed that story, not deep down. It just wasn't Joss.' She gave Jenna a beseeching look. 'Tell me about Cornwall. What's he been doing down there?'

'Painting, mostly . . . no, I'll qualify that . . . exclusively painting. He's finished quite a few canvases. And they're really good. Joss definitely has talent.'

'But he can paint here at home,' Francine protested.

It was Jenna's turn to sigh. 'He feels that if he comes home, then he'll be forced back into the business. It's understandable that Isaac wants his son here to take over from him, but the thing is, Joss isn't yet ready for that. He just needs to think it all out for himself.' She gave Francine an encouraging smile. 'Give it time. He'll make the right decision. I'm sure of it.'

Jenna described her meeting with Joss, leaving nothing out, and Francine's brows shot up when she described his rented cottage. She told her about Vincent Pemberley-Jones's exhibition and her encounter with Victoria.

Francine groaned. 'She's a man-eater, that one; but if she's found somebody new in Cornwall, then at least she's out of Gil's hair.'

At the mention of Gil's name, Jenna sat up. 'She has no claim on him.' She saw Francine's quick glance. But she had no reason to hide her feelings for Gil. They were both free agents. 'We've been seeing a bit of each other in Cornwall,' she admitted, her mouth curving in a self-conscious grin. 'I like him.'

Francine watched her for a long time, and then nodded. 'You make a good couple,' she said. 'But look out for that little madam. I only met her a couple of times. Molly and Isaac are friendly with her parents, and she came to dinner a couple of times with them. She set her cap at Gil straight away. He did well to stay out of that one's clutches.'

The mention of Victoria's name had unsettled Jenna. It seemed that people were lining up to warn her about the girl, but she refused to be intimidated by the woman's fantasies. Gil was not interested!

Francine declined Jenna's offer to take the twins to their afternoon nursery session, insisting the air would do her good. 'We have an au pair now to help with the children,' she explained, 'but I've given her some time off.' She sighed. 'I can't stop worrying about Joss and his father, but at least I can get the children away from Fenfleet for a few hours. You should do the same, Jenna.'

After Francine and the children left, Jenna went back to the house and began to wander around the familiar rooms. There was no shortage of paintings and sculptures, but nothing of Joss's work. Surely he would have painted something special for his parents? Why was it not on display?

The sound of distant chatter led her to the kitchen. 'Come away in, lass. We're all through here,' a rich Yorkshire voice called out from behind the door. The large and comfortable Esme, the cook; Dan, her gardener husband; and Maria, the maid who had brought their lunch, were seated around the kitchen table drinking tea.

Esme's chins wobbled, and her round, apple-red cheeks stretched into a smile as she beckoned Jenna forward. 'Many a scone we've made at this table, lass, do you remember?'

Jenna nodded, grinning. 'I had my own special apron with my name on it. You made it for me, Esme.'

'I did, Jenna lass,' she sighed, and her eyes glistened with unshed tears. 'Will he be alright . . . Mr Isaac?'

Jenna went to put her arms around Esme. 'Of course he will. Uncle Isaac's had to deal with worse than this. He always comes sailing through.' She looked round the three worried faces. 'You all know that.' She hoped she was sounding more confident than she felt.

Dan cleared his throat and stood up. His sandy hair was now speckled with grey. 'You should get out for some fresh air, Miss. I could take you on a tour of the garden if you like.' His weather-beaten face creased into a smile. 'What d'you think?'

Jenna gave a smiling nod round the table. As she turned to follow him out, Esme called after her, 'Can you still ride a bicycle, lass?'

The question took Jenna by surprise, but she nodded. It had been years since she'd been in a saddle. The thought sparked an instant recall of hot summer days when she, Joss and Francine had cycled miles along the country lanes and up into the North York Moors.

'Isn't that old shopping cycle still in one of the outhouses, Dan? Maybe Jenna here would like to take it out for a spin instead.'

Dan shot her a questioning look, and Jenna shrugged. 'Why not? Sounds like a great idea.'

The ladies' cycle that Dan wheeled out of the low brick outhouse looked in much better condition than Jenna had been expecting. There was even a helmet in the basket.

She thanked him, and watched him lumber off, pleased that he hadn't stayed to watch her first wobbly attempts to stay upright. But after a few tries the technique came back to her, and moments later she was cycling through the garden and out the back gate. It was the last thing she had expected to be doing today, but now that she'd got the hang of cycling again, she was enjoying herself.

The lanes behind Fenfleet were narrower and more overgrown than those on the other side of the house. The hedges here were high, and every now and then there were gaps through which Jenna caught glimpses of cows and sheep sharing the same fields. She sailed past a row of horse chestnut trees, and had a sudden memory of Joss, as a schoolboy, getting stuck in the high branches, and Isaac having to fetch a ladder to rescue him. The memory made her shiver and she wondered again how they were all getting on at the hospital. Would Isaac's condition have improved, or . . . ? She couldn't bear to think about the alternative. Her mobile phone was in her pocket, but neither Gil nor Joss had so far called her. Surely they would have if the news was bad? She swallowed back the lump in her throat and sent up a silent prayer.

She'd reached a crossroads, and stopped to examine the signpost. It offered a choice of two villages. She decided to cycle to the closest one, which was half a mile away.

Fenfleet was much as she had remembered: a pleasant, rambling village with a wide main street, a general store and a pub. She didn't see the big green 4×4 until it raced past at such a speed that her bicycle wobbled. The machine went in one direction and Jenna flew off in another, landing in a painful heap at the side of the road. She rubbed her grazed knee, glaring up at the errant driver. He had stopped and was hurrying back. A pair of concerned blue eyes gazed down at her.

'I'm so sorry,' the young man said, helping Jenna to her feet. 'I should never have been driving so fast through the village. Are you alright?'

Jenna struggled up and brushed down the jeans and navy top she'd changed into earlier. There was a tear at the knee and traces of blood.

'No thanks to you,' she snapped. 'You were going like a bat out of hell. Is this how people around here behave now?'

The young man was looking suitably ashamed. 'I really am sorry.' He shot a glance across to the pub. 'Look, let me make amends. Let me buy you a drink.' He thrust out a hand. 'Guy Bradford,' he said. 'Pleased to meet you.'

She muttered her own name and bent to retrieve the cycle, staring in dismay at the buckled wheel. 'It's not even mine,' she wailed.

Guy grabbed the bicycle and heaved

it into the back of his vehicle. 'I'll buy whoever it belongs to a new one,' he offered, his voice still apologetic. He'd taken her arm and was leading her across the road.

'Just a minute. What did you say your name was?'

He repeated it, still steering her in the direction of the pub. 'We haven't met previously or anything, have we?' He was grinning, his sights still set on the Red Lion.

Jenna was seething inside. This was the man who had tried to cause trouble by suggesting to Francine that Joss had gone off with another woman.

He was ignoring her struggle to free herself. 'Drink first,' he insisted. 'Then I'll take you straight home.'

Judging by the smiles and nods that came his way, everybody in the pub seemed to know him. And Jenna didn't miss the curious glances that came her way. She studied him as he stood at the bar waiting for their drinks. He looked about the same height and build as Gil, but his hair was blond, short and decidedly crinkly. And, judging by his white clothes, he was on his way to take part in a cricket match.

'I take it you don't live around here?' He'd come back and had placed their drinks on their table before sliding into the seat beside her.

'I'm staying with friends,' Jenna said, curtly.

'Do I know them?'

'How should I know who you are acquainted with?' She didn't like him, but maybe he really was doing his best to make amends, so she relented. 'I'm staying at Fenfleet. I think you know it.'

Guy's teasing blue eyes narrowed. 'That old dog,' he said. 'Trust Joss Maitland to pick a looker.' He gave her a sly grin. 'I trust it *is* Joss you're with and not that other chap, Ryder?'

Jenna stared at him. 'I'm not *with* anybody, at least not in the way you're suggesting. But, if you must know, I came up from Cornwall this morning with Joss. His father's ill.'

'Yes, I heard,' Guy said, frowning. 'Word spreads fast around these parts. How is Isaac?'

'I don't really know. They're all at the hospital now.'

'Hmm, that was a bit of bad luck,' Guy said. 'But the Maitlands are a tough bunch. I'm sure old Isaac will be fine.'

Jenna wished she could share his confidence.

He was studying her over his glass, making her feel uncomfortable. 'On second thoughts,' he said, 'you're probably more Ryder's type. He can pick 'em. Take that little piece he got mixed up with . . . '

Jenna's brows came down. 'What do you mean?'

Guy's smile was full of malice. 'I was thinking of the willowy blonde. One minute they had split up, and the next they're back together again.'

Jenna's back stiffened. What rubbish was he talking?

'Victoria, wasn't it?' He lifted his glass and took a deep swig of the lager, then used the back of his hand to wipe foam from his mouth. 'She was quite a hit when Ryder brought her here, I can tell you.'

Fingers of ice gripped Jenna's heart. Had Gil misled her about his relationship with Victoria? If he disliked her so much, then why was he taking her for cosy drinks at the local pub? She felt numb.

All the way back to Fenfleet, Guy kept up a stream of chatter, but Jenna wasn't listening. There could be any number of reasons why Gil would take Victoria for a drink. She was getting things out of proportion.

It was early evening when Gil and the others got back from the hospital. Jenna had steeled herself for bad news, but the looks on their faces suggested an improvement in Isaac's condition.

Ignoring Gil, Jenna ran to meet Molly and Joss at the front door. Molly caught her hand. 'Isaac is a lot better,' she said, her eyes shining.

Jenna clasped a hand to her chest, feeling the relief flooding through her.

'That's wonderful news.'

'It's early days yet, but the doctors are very pleased with him,' Molly said, turning to touch Joss's arm. 'Your father was so happy to see you.'

It wasn't easy to avoid Gil's eyes. No matter how hard she tried, she could still see that look of hurt puzzlement. But what could he expect when he had lied about Victoria?

Molly had locked arms with her and Joss, and was marching them into the sitting room, calling for Gil to join them. 'We all need a good strong cup of tea,' she announced.

Out of the corner of her eye, Jenna could see Gil watching her, but she did her best to avoid his gaze.

By mutual consent, no one changed for dinner that evening. Francine joined them, leaving the children in the capable hands of their au pair. The meal was informal and Molly was animated, talking non-stop about her husband and how good it was to have Joss home again. But both men seemed unexpectedly quiet, and Jenna wondered if they had quarrelled.

As they rose from the table after dinner, Jenna was on the point of excusing herself for an early night when Molly said, 'Perhaps Jenna would like to see the garden. Why don't you show her around, Gil? It's not as though you have to go back to that cottage.' She smiled across at Jenna. 'Gil is staying at Fenfleet for a few days. I don't think he trusted me here on my own.'

'Maybe Jenna's too tired to see the garden tonight,' Gil said.

'On the contrary.' Jenna forced a smile. 'That's a lovely idea.'

Dusk was falling when they went outside, but the warmth of the day still lingered. The air was heavy with the scent of roses and honeysuckle. Jenna trailed a hand over the fragrant bushes. 'It's peaceful out here,' she said, her voice hardly more than a whisper.

'They've got Dan to thank for that. He's Fenfleet's gardener — amongst a million other things, I understand.'

Jenna nodded. 'We're old friends.'

She had no intention of telling him about her cycling adventure and her meeting with Guy Bradford — or anything else that had happened that afternoon. That would come later. Right now, it wasn't her feelings that were important. 'Is Isaac really improving as much as Molly says?'

For the first time since they had returned from the hospital, Gil seemed to relax. 'He's got a way to go yet, but yes . . . it really does seem so. It's what happens later I'm worried about.'

Jenna looked at him, waiting for him to go on.

He frowned. 'Molly and Isaac think Joss is back for good. They don't realize he's planning to get back to Cornwall just as soon as he can.'

Jenna stared accusingly at him. 'What makes them think that? You didn't tell them he was home for good, did you, Gil?'

He rounded on her. 'Of course not. I'm hardly likely to do that. But it's not surprising that they made the assumption. Isaac will obviously have to take things more easily when he eventually gets home. I suppose he and Molly have been thinking Joss would step into Isaac's shoes and work alongside me overseeing the stores.'

Jenna sighed. Her family's worries were not over yet.

Gil snapped a piece of branch from one of the shrubs and began plucking off leaves, unconsciously discarding them over the gravel path. 'Is it my imagination, Jenna, or have you been avoiding me since we came back from the hospital?'

This was her chance to challenge him about his date with Victoria — but what would be the point? Whatever there had been between them was in the past. It was *her* that Gil wanted now.

She shrugged. 'Sorry, I've just been feeling a bit out of sorts.'

'Well, we will have to put that right,' Gil said softly, pulling her into his arms. His mouth came down on hers before Jenna realized what was happening. His kiss was so tender that Jenna thought her heart would stop. Every cell in her body was urging abandonment to his kiss — and she was powerless to resist.

Later, out of sight of the house, as they strolled hand in hand in the growing darkness, Gil asked, 'Do you really think Joss plans to go rushing back to Cornwall under the circumstances?'

'I think Joss will do what's right, and at the moment that will be looking after his family, and making sure Isaac's recovery is as stress-free as possible.' She pursed her lips and looked up at him. 'That doesn't mean he will give up his painting — and I don't think he should, not when he is so talented. I've already told him what a good artist he is. He could certainly make a living from it.'

Gil raised a hand. 'You don't have to go on. I'm getting the picture,' he said, grimly.

The night air was getting chilly and they headed back to the house. Jenna stifled a yawn, suddenly realizing how exhausted she was. It had been a long day, and now all she wanted to do was to sleep.

'An early night for you, my girl,' Gil said, eyeing her. 'You and I have a busy day tomorrow.'

Jenna raised an eyebrow.

'You'll see.' He grinned in answer to her silent question, and touched the tip of her nose with his finger, as one would a child's. 'I'll tell you all about it in the morning.'

Jenna called 'goodnight' to Joss and Molly, who appeared to be still deep in conversation in the dining room, and headed upstairs. She tried ringing her father again, but his phone was still switched off. She knew he hated his mobile phone and had only agreed to have one because Jenna had insisted. But what was the point if he didn't switch it on? She felt irritated. She'd call the gallery in the morning to find out what was happening.

Under the shower, she let the warm rivulets of water ease away the traumas of the day. She didn't want to think any more about the sly, green-eyed Victoria. Gil would have had a good reason for taking her to the pub. But she'd have to think about all that later. Right now she was deadly tired, and all she wanted to do was drift off to sleep, still tasting the sweetness of Gil's kiss on her lips.

The sounds of movement in the corridor outside her door woke Jenna early next morning. There was a quiet tap, the door opened, and Maria breezed in carrying a small silver tray.

'Mrs Maitland thought you would like some tea.' She smiled, laying down the tray on the bedside chest before going to the window to draw back the heavy green drapes.

Jenna screwed up her eyes against the sudden light and stretched. 'Thank you, Maria,' she said. She could get used to this.

The whole family was in the breakfast room when Jenna walked in. Molly was at the head of the table, with Joss and Francine on either side, and Charlotte and Alfie beside their mother, tucking into plates of cereal. The way Gil's eyes lit up when he saw her sent a bolt of pleasure down her spine.

'The poached fish is particularly good this morning,' Molly said.

But Jenna noticed she had hardly touched her own plate of food.

'I thought I'd call in at the York store this morning,' Gil announced, laying down his cutlery and easing his empty plate away.

Molly nodded. 'Good idea. Isaac wouldn't want us neglecting the business. She smiled across at Jenna. 'Perhaps Jenna would like to join you. I'm sure she'd be bored to pieces rattling around this old place all day.'

Gil raised an eyebrow. 'Well, that was the plan. But what do you think, Jenna?'

'Only if I can visit Isaac in hospital at some point. I've come all the way from Cornwall and I haven't seen him yet.'

'That's my fault,' Francine said. 'If I hadn't taken up all your time yesterday, you could have gone to visit him with the others.'

'We could do both,' Gil cut in. 'There's no reason why we can't call in on Isaac later.'

'Good idea,' Molly said. 'Isaac's been asking for you, Jenna.'

'Tell him I'll be there,' Jenna laughed.

An hour later she was in Gil's green sports car, and they were threading their way through the city traffic.

Maitlands Department Store was three floors high and occupied a prime corner site right in the busy city centre. Gil drove through the side arch and punched in a code to open the electronically-controlled gates to the small private car park. They entered the store by a back door, as Jenna had done so many times before, took the lift to the top floor, and then walked along the familiar green-carpeted corridor to Gil's office. He'd taken the one next to Isaac's. It had once been hers.

She glanced around, pleased to see that nothing much had changed. The room was large with small attic windows that looked out over the red-pantiled city roofs. At the far side, towering above everything, was York Minster. It was Jenna's favourite view of the city. As she gazed out, another door into the office opened and a middle-aged woman, her brown hair scraped back into a tight bun, bustled in, giving Jenna a brief nod as she swept past and placed an open diary on Gil's desk. Then she stopped and turned back to peer over her spectacles at Jenna.

'It can't be . . . Miss Maitland?'

Jenna extended her hand, laughing. 'Yes, Jane, it's me. How are you?'

'Well, I almost didn't recognize you.' She tilted her head and studied Jenna. 'What's happened to the shy little schoolgirl Mr Isaac used to bring into the office? You look so . . . different.'

Jenna coloured. 'I've grown up, Jane. But I did used to work here. It wasn't that long ago.' Out of the corner of her eye she could see Gil was grinning.

But Jane Harper hadn't finished. 'You've blossomed, Jenna, if might say so — and you've caught the sun.'

Gil cleared his throat. 'Have I missed much since I've been away?'

Miss Harper switched her attention back to her boss. 'Mr Bradley has taken over all the appointments as you instructed, Mr Ryder,' she said briskly. 'I think it's all running quite smoothly.'

Jenna detected a smug smile.

'Thank you, Jane. I knew we could depend on you and William.' He turned to Jenna. 'I see you two know each other.'

Jenna nodded. 'Miss Harper has been the backbone of Maitlands for as long as I can remember.'

'Twenty-four years next Christmas,' Jane Harper interrupted.

Gil smiled. 'And everyone knows that the place would crash around us if she wasn't here.'

The woman reddened at the compliment, then her eyes behind the round-rimmed spectacles grew serious. 'How is Mr Isaac?' she asked, her voice hesitant. 'We've all been so worried.'

Jenna could see the woman's concern was genuine.

'There was a bit of an improvement last night, and the doctors told Mrs Maitland this morning that they are pleased with him.'

Miss Harper let out a heartfelt sigh, a hand at her throat. 'I can't tell you how glad I am to hear that.'

As she turned to go, Gil called after her, 'I'll tell him you were asking.'

The secretary turned and nodded before leaving the room, smiling.

'She's always been devoted to Isaac,' Jenna said. 'I always suspected she might be a little in love with him.'

Gil was scanning the appointments diary, flicking through pages, checking dates. 'William Bradley seems to have everything in hand,' he murmured with a satisfied nod. 'He's still Isaac's right-hand man when I'm not around . . . and, judging by this, we have nothing immediate to worry about.'

He closed the book and walked round the big wooden desk to take Jenna's arm. 'Fancy a trip down memory lane?' he grinned, steering her out of the door, past the lift and down the stairs to the second floor.

Jenna glanced around at the displays of swimwear, golfing equipment and tennis rackets. She could even see a leather saddle and other riding equipment at the far end of the shop floor. This was new, and she suspected it was Gil's influence. The old buzz she always got from being on the shop floor was coming back. She could feel the tingle of excitement shooting through her as they walked.

'You'll remember our leisure department,' Gil said with a flourish.

They walked through the displays, being waylaid at every turn by anxious members of staff requesting updates on Isaac Maitland's condition. Jenna was pleased that so many of them still remembered her. She noticed Gil knew everyone by name, and admired the way he took time to stop and pass on the latest news. By the time they had reached the perfumery and fashion departments on the ground floor it was obvious just how much affection this workforce had, not just for the Maitlands, but for Gil too. Somehow she wasn't surprised.

Once they had negotiated their way through the glass doors and out onto the busy street, Gil spread his arms and grinned. 'Well, Madam, I'm at your command. What would you like to see?'

Jenna spun round, laughing, taking in the historic old buildings, then her eyes widened and she pointed. 'There,' she said. 'That's where I'd like to go.'

Gil pursed his lips in a considered way and nodded. 'The Minster . . . Good choice.'

Hand in hand, they threaded their way through the crowds of sightseers and shoppers, and ran up the few steps that took them into the magnificent old cathedral. In the street outside, traffic continued to hurtle over the ancient cobbles, and people were still hurrying about their business. But here, under the Minster's vaulted ceilings and magnificent stained-glass windows, all was peaceful. In a far corner Jenna could see a class of schoolchildren earnestly bent over their sketching pads, trying to capture the grandeur of the place.

'It's amazing,' Jenna breathed, her eyes wide. 'I've always been in awe of this place.'

Gil led her through the building, stopping to point out a round stained-glass window high above them. 'This section had to be rebuilt after it was destroyed by a fire in the 1980s. Would you believe, it was struck by a bolt of lightning?'

Jenna knew the story, but Gil was obviously enjoying telling it, and she wasn't about to spoil his fun. She stared up at the beautiful window. 'Surely no-one could rebuild that?'

'I think I read somewhere that it was badly cracked by the heat, but it stayed in one piece,' Gil said. 'But it was an incredible restoration job to get it back looking like that.'

Jenna nodded, matching his slow pace through the building. Then he whispered in her ear, 'I've saved the best bit for last. How is your head for heights?'

'I find high places exhilarating,' she laughed. 'But what are you up to?'

He took her hand and strode across the ancient flagged floor to a small door in a corner. 'Follow me,' he instructed, guiding her through to the foot of a narrow stone spiral staircase. He extended his hand upwards. 'To the tower!' he said, his eyes twinkling mischievously.

Jenna squinted up the dark twisting stairs. 'You're not serious?'

'Of course,' he said. 'It'll be fun.'

Her brow creased. 'How many of these steps are there?'

'I'll tell you when we reach the top.' He grinned.

Jenna laughed and shook her head. 'You're sure it's safe?'

Just as he was about to answer, a middle-aged couple appeared from above and squeezed past them.

'It's a long way up,' the woman

confided, smiling. 'I hope you're fit.'

Jenna thought about how great the view would be from the top, and made up her mind. 'Let's do it,' she said.

The winding stairs seemed to go on forever and her legs were aching. 'How much further?' she puffed.

'Almost there,' Gil said, encouragingly.

By the time they stepped out into the sunshine, Jenna's knees were knocking, but she gasped when she saw her surroundings.

'This is the best view of the city,' Gil said, pointing out over the rooftops towards the Yorkshire Wolds. 'And down there is the river. We can go out on a boat later, if you like.'

She nodded her approval, then asked, 'How high up are we?'

'I'm not sure, but we've just climbed almost three hundred steps to get here.'

The wind was strong at this height and Jenna gripped the safety rail. Far below, she could see people scurrying around like tiny ants. Gil moved closer, and she rested her head against his chest. She could feel his heart pounding beneath her cheek as he put his arms around her. Their narrow ledge high up on top of the tower suddenly felt like the safest place in the world. His fingers stroked her hair then strayed to her face, tilting her chin up, forcing her to gaze into the dark depths of those melting brown eyes. She touched her fingers to his mouth, and then his lips brushed hers. She had to grip the rail again to steady herself.

'I think we should go back down,' she whispered, breathlessly.

He laughed. 'I thought you had a head for heights?'

Jenna glanced around her. Physical heights weren't the problem, she thought, with a secret grin. It was the other sort that was so unpredictable.

Back at ground level, they wandered arm in arm through York's maze of cobbled streets, stopping occasionally to gaze into the windows of the specialist shops and quirky boutiques. They went into a teashop and ordered hot buttered teacakes, and laughed as they wiped dripping butter from each other's chins.

As they got up to leave, Jenna glanced across at a couple of women chatting — and froze. The long blonde hair was familiar. *Please don't let it be Victoria*, she pleaded silently. The woman turned and stared directly at her. She was a complete stranger. Jenna took a deep breath, hoping Gil hadn't noticed the incident.

She was becoming obsessed with the woman.

On the narrow pavement outside, she forced a smile. 'Where is this river, then?' she said. Her voice sounded strange and she knew Gil was giving her a curious look, but she ignored it. She was determined not to let thoughts of Victoria spoil this day.

12

Jenna was shocked when she saw how pitifully tired Isaac looked. His skin against the white hospital linen was the colour of fine parchment. This wasn't the strident six-feet-two dynamo of a man she knew. Illness had taken its toll, but his eyes lit up when he caught sight of Jenna and his arms went out to hug her. She rushed into them.

'Uncle Isaac, what have you been doing to yourself?' Her voice was teasing and he responded with a crooked grin.

'This is what happens when you're not here to keep me in line, young Jenna. But I'll be back on my feet soon and giving them all a run for their money again.' He patted the bed. 'Sit here beside me, lass, you're a sight for sore eyes.'

Jenna did as he asked, studying the

familiar craggy face. He was thinner, but the blue eyes still twinkled.

Jenna sent Molly a conspiratorial wink before narrowing her eyes. 'Are you behaving yourself in here, Uncle Isaac?'

'If you mean, am I chatting up the nurses, well . . . shame on you, Jenna Maitland. I would never do such a thing.'

'He's fibbing,' said a voice from the door as a pretty young nurse popped her head round. 'This man's the biggest charmer on the ward, but he does need his beauty sleep. So just another five minutes, folks, then I'll have to ask you to leave.'

Her tone was light, but all of them knew they were being warned not to overtire the patient. When he realized the visit was coming to an end, Isaac struggled to sit up, but Molly placed a firm hand on his shoulder.

'I don't think that's a good idea, darling.'

But her husband ignored the advice, turning to Gil. 'I'm told you've been to the store?' The question was an invitation to give him a run-down on how his business was progressing in his absence.

But Gil only nodded. 'I have,' he said, 'and William and Miss Harper have everything under control.'

Isaac Maitland lifted an eyebrow at Jenna, inviting her to confirm this. She nodded. 'Gil's right, Isaac. Everything seems to be running like clockwork.' She thought she saw a fleeting hint of disappointment, so she added, 'I've never known so many people to be anxious about their boss's health.'

She could feel Molly's eyes on her, and wondered if she'd said the wrong thing. But Isaac was beaming.

'That's right,' Gil cut in. 'It took twice as long just to get through the store this morning because we had to make so many stops to assure people you were doing well.'

'You should have told them I'll be back cracking that whip again sooner than they know,' Isaac said, but his normally robust voice sounded weak.

'You're tired, dear. We'll let you get some rest now,' Molly said, patting her husband's shoulder.

Jenna gave a final wave and followed Gil and Joss as they made a tactful exit to give the Maitlands a few moments of privacy before visiting time was up. In the corridor, Joss looked from one to the other.

'Had a nice day?'

Jenna felt her cheeks grow hot and was instantly annoyed with herself. She'd every right to spend time with whomever she chose.

But Gil's eyebrows had come down in a scowl. 'Do you have a problem with that?'

Jenna was about to step between them when Joss raised his hands in a gesture of defence. 'Just a comment,' he said with a grin. 'Why so touchy?'

Gil cleared his throat and glared at Joss. 'We have to talk . . . not here, but later . . . there are things we need to sort out.'

Jenna felt the first stirrings of unease. Was Gil going to insist that Joss should play his part in the running of the family business? She could sense trouble.

When Molly met them in the car park a few minutes later, she was beaming. 'He looks so much better, more like his old self again.' She touched Jenna's hand. 'Thanks for coming — and for teasing him. You brought the smile back to his face.'

Then, turning to Gil, she announced she would go back in his car, leaving Jenna to return to Fenfleet in Isaac's big silver-and-black four-wheel drive with Joss. It was the busiest time on the city's roads and traffic was heavy as they headed for the ring road. Apparently not in a mood for talking, Joss stared at the slowly-moving vehicles ahead. Jenna stayed quiet for as long as she could, but the silence was becoming uncomfortable. She glanced at him, but his profile was rigid.

Keep it light, she told herself, and

said, 'This is a bit better than that old boneshaker you were driving in Cornwall.' She saw him frown, then his mouth twitched into a smile.

'I'll have you know, I love that old Jeep.'

Jenna laughed. She had to admit she had developed a sneaking affection for it herself.

'But I'm beginning to wonder if I'll ever see it again.' A serious note had crept into his voice.

She avoided glancing at him. 'Does that mean you've decided to stay on here in Yorkshire?'

He shrugged. 'I don't know yet what my long-term plans are, but I obviously won't be leaving before Dad's back on his feet.' He kept his eyes on the road as the traffic inched towards the roundabout where they had to turn off for Fenfleet. 'Gil's been pointing out a few home truths about my responsibilities here. And he's right, even if I don't appreciate being told.' He let out a long, exasperated sigh. 'If only I could put everything on hold and just deal with what's happening now. But they won't let me do that. Everyone wants answers, and I don't have any.'

Jenna touched his arm. 'You can't really blame them, Joss, but you're right. The family — and I mean all of us — have to deal with what's happening now. If we can keep things ticking over at the stores, then that should be our goal for the moment. There will be plenty of time to sort things out when Isaac gets home.'

Joss was smiling and she stared at him, frowning. 'Did I say something funny?'

He shook his head. 'I thought you'd given up any idea of being part of the business. Am I right in suspecting I was wrong?' He glanced across at her. 'We all know how brilliant you were. You used to run the York store almost single-handed.'

Jenna laughed. 'That's a slight exaggeration. But I always felt quite proud that Isaac trusted me as much as he did. I appreciated the responsibility.'

'Then come back. Daniel can manage the gallery on his own now. It's here in Yorkshire that you're needed.'

Jenna's mouth dropped open. 'Are you suggesting I offer my services to Isaac again?' She shook her head. 'I'm not saying I wouldn't love to come back to Yorkshire, but you're wrong about Dad. He really does need me.'

Joss shrugged. 'Maybe he did, but that was two years ago. We all know Daniel's gallery wouldn't have survived if you hadn't gone down to London to run it for him. But don't you think it's time he took some responsibility? It is his business, after all.'

Jenna stared at him. 'Isn't that what Molly and Isaac have been saying about you?'

'Well, exactly . . . which is why I'm giving the whole thing so much thought. But you have to do that too, Jenna. I might have inherited your dad's artistic gene, but you got Isaac's flair for business. It would be a shame to waste it on a tiny London gallery when you're capable of so much more.'

She sank back in her seat, staring ahead. It was true her father had shares in the Maitland empire, and that one day they would come to her. But when she moved to London, she had more or less given up on her dreams of any further hands-on involvement in the company. Molly and Isaac might even think her presumptuous if she suggested it now.

They'd reached the high stone pillars at the entrance to Fenfleet. Joss turned in, the car's tyres crunching on the gravelled drive.

'You weren't seriously suggesting I should come back, were you, Joss?' The idea had shaken her.

Just ahead of them, Molly and Gil were getting out of the car. Joss sat watching them for a moment, then said, quietly, 'Of course not. Forget I spoke. I know you have your commitments in London and you won't let your father down.'

They followed Molly and Gil into the house. The mention of her father reminded her that she still hadn't heard from him. She'd meant to ring the gallery, but so much had happened that day. When she got to her room she sat on the bed with her mobile, scrolling down to her father's number.

'At last,' she said when he answered. 'I've been trying to reach you for two days. Where have you been, Dad?'

'Spain,' he said. 'I've been invited to exhibit at a gallery in Madrid. They wanted me out there to go over the details.'

'Well, you should have stayed in touch. It's Uncle Isaac. He's had a heart attack.'

She heard the intake of breath at the other end. 'Is he OK?'

'I think he's getting there, but it was touch and go for a while.'

'I'm sorry, love.' He sounded shocked. 'You're right. I'd no business taking off like that without letting you know. How is Molly bearing up?'

'I think she would appreciate a call from you.'

'I'll do it now,' he said. 'And what about you, Jenna? Are you OK?'

'Yes, Dad.' She smiled into the phone. 'I'm fine. Just keep your phone switched on, will you?'

Jenna felt better after talking to her father, but Joss was right. He felt no responsibility for his business — not when he had her to run it for him.

Everyone was in a light-hearted mood when Jenna joined them in the drawing room. Francine was wearing a loose cotton dress in a pink that suited her blue eyes and creamy complexion. Gil and Joss were in lightweight suits. Molly had chosen a green silk blouse and cream slacks.

Francine linked arms with Jenna and they went together into the dining room. 'I'm having an evening of freedom,' she confided. 'The twins are being put to bed by our au pair, Caterina. I don't think you've met her. She's an absolute treasure.'

Jenna was pleased to see how relaxed Francine and Joss now appeared, and she didn't miss the private glances that passed between the couple throughout the meal.

They'd been about to move to the drawing room for coffee when Maria knocked and entered. 'It's Miss Symington,' she addressed Molly. 'She wants to see you.'

Jenna froze. Victoria! What was she doing here? She glanced across the table at Gil. His expression was like stone.

But the visitor wasn't waiting to be invited in. The dining room door flew open and Victoria, her long blonde hair streaming behind her, flew in, arms outstretched, and made a beeline for Molly.

'I'm so sorry,' she cried, breathlessly. 'I've just heard about Isaac.' She kissed her cheek and Jenna saw Molly stiffen.

'He gave us all a fright, but he's improving now,' she said, an edge to her voice.

'Well, thank heavens for that.' The blonde eyelashes fluttered in Gil's direction. 'We don't want anything nasty happening to my *second* favourite man,' Victoria cooed.

Jenna registered the skimpy red top, figure-hugging black miniskirt and matching high suede boots, and watched with growing disbelief as she rushed into Gil's arms and kissed him.

Avoiding Jenna's stare, he disentangled himself. 'Victoria.' He cleared his throat. 'What are you doing here?'

'You should have called me, darling,' she accused, her confident green eyes scanning the faces round the table. 'Cornwall is only just down the road. I would have flown back immediately if I'd known.'

'You were in Cornwall?' There was astonishment in Molly's voice.

Victoria turned to Joss. 'Didn't you tell your mother, darling? Joss gave me a lift down a couple of weeks ago. I'm surprised you didn't know.'

Gil gave a nervous cough as the woman fixed her stare on Jenna.

'You two haven't met,' he started, making a poor job of hiding his anger. 'Jenna Maitland, meet Victoria Symington.'

Jenna stared, waiting for the girl's announcement that they had already met — the last time in Pemberley-Jones's bedroom. But, to her surprise, Victoria offered a limp hand. 'I'm Gil's girlfriend,' she said.

For a few seconds no one spoke. Joss and Francine exchanged an embarrassed look. Jenna's patience was becoming exhausted.

'You know that's not true, Victoria,' Gil said, his eyes blazing.

Victoria put the tips of her fingers to her mouth and gazed around the room with wide, innocent eyes. 'Did I say 'girlfriend'? I meant 'friend'.' She put out a hand to touch his face. 'Forever friends, eh, Gil? Isn't that what we agreed?'

Gil brushed her hand away as Molly gestured towards the adjoining drawing room. 'We were just about to have coffee, Victoria; perhaps you would like to join us.' There was a sharp edge to her voice that Jenna hadn't heard before.

Maybe Victoria sensed it, for she flashed Molly a smile. 'I'd love to, but I'll have to get back. Mummy and Daddy have delayed dinner for me, so they'll be waiting.' She gave Gil a final peck on the cheek and gazed into his eyes. 'As soon as I heard about Isaac, I dropped everything and just rushed over here. You will keep me updated, darling . . . won't you?'

Gil glared at her, and Jenna saw Victoria's elegant eyebrow arch just a fraction. 'OK, fine,' she said, looking round the table. 'I'll see you all later, then.'

The door closed behind her and Joss let out a loud sigh and stretched his long legs under the table. 'Well, Gil,' he said. 'You have your work cut out for you there.'

All eyes were on Gil and he gave a helpless shrug. 'I can't help it if she lives nearby,' he said. He was looking at Jenna.

'A very high-spirited neighbour,' Joss quipped.

Molly pushed back her chair and stood up, her face grim. 'I think you need an urgent talk with that young woman, Gil.'

She moved to leave the room, and then turned back, beckoning Jenna to join her. 'I haven't shown you the additions to my collection of Wemyss, have I? Are you still interested in pottery, my dear?'

Jenna nodded, dumbly; they frequently exhibited ceramics and sculptures in her father's gallery. But the last few minutes had stunned her.

'Some of the new stuff is quite rare,' Molly was saying as she steered Jenna into the other room. 'I would appreciate your opinion.'

When they were out of earshot of the men, she said, 'You don't want to pay too much attention to Victoria. She's a spoiled only child who wants for nothing.' Molly

251

pursed her lips and frowned. 'I'm afraid she is used to getting her own way. We were all a bit amused at first when she set her sights on Gil. Well, it's not as though a good-looking man like him wouldn't be used to coping with smitten young women.'

They were crossing the main hall to the smaller room where Molly's collection of Wemyss was displayed. 'They only went out a couple of times, as I remember, but she used to pester him with calls and text messages. She just wouldn't leave him alone.' She sighed. 'We couldn't be too rude to her because Isaac and I are friendly with her parents.'

'I don't remember a Symington family living near here.' Jenna frowned.

'They came after you went to London.' Molly's intelligent blue eyes gazed into the distance as she remembered. 'Victoria came to dinner with her parents one evening about eighteen months ago, when Gil was here. I think she set her sights on landing him from the moment they met. I suppose poor Gil was just beaten into submission. I always suspected she fancied running our fashion departments, and saw her friendship with him as a way in.'

Jenna thought of the girl's trendy clothes and her overconfident, bossy manner. There was no doubt she would be in her element ruling the roost in the Maitlands' stores. She wondered what the staff would have to say about that.

'Victoria strikes me as someone who knows how to get her own way.' She slid Molly a look. 'From what you've just told me, I can't see her giving up on Gil.'

'She's not for Gil,' Molly said. 'I trust his judgment. He'll find the right girl, and when he does, he'll stick with her.'

Somewhere deep inside Jenna, a tiny chink of joy had started to grow, and she smiled at Molly.

The older woman's eyes twinkled as she glanced around her precious pottery collection. 'What do you think?' she asked.

Jenna strolled round, inspecting the delicate baskets painted with pink dog roses, the preserve jars with their luscious dark plums, and numerous assorted mugs. She knew Molly would have paid over a thousand for most of these items. Then she stopped in front of a chunky pig. 'May I?' she asked, reaching to pick it up for closer inspection.

Molly nodded. 'I wondered if you would spot that one,' she said, her eyes shining with pride. 'It's a Plichta pig, and very rare.'

Jenna turned it over and saw it was signed by Joseph Nekola, son of the company's founding designer, Karel Nekola, which dated it to around the nineteen-thirties. She'd seen one similar sold in a London auction house, but couldn't remember how many thousands of pounds the successful bidder had to spend. Perhaps it had been Molly Maitland.

'It's a wonderful collection.' She smiled, genuinely impressed.

'Hmm.' Molly nodded, casting one last wistful look around the room. 'Isaac buys me a new piece every year on my birthday.'

The smell of freshly-brewed coffee was drifting through from the other room as Molly added, 'Why don't you come with me tomorrow, Jenna? You could pop in and say a brief hello to Isaac, then spend the morning shopping in York. We could meet up for lunch later.'

The invitation surprised Jenna, but the more she considered it, the more the idea appealed to her. She'd had so little time on her own recently, and she had a lot of serious thinking to do. 'That's a lovely idea, Molly. Thank you, I'd love it.'

'Right, that's settled then.' Molly smiled as they strolled back to join the others.

'Jenna's coming into York with me in the morning,' she announced as they walked into the room. 'Gil, I thought maybe you and Joss could call in at the stores . . . just to make sure everything is running smoothly.'

The men stared at her, then Joss frowned. For a second, Jenna thought he was going to refuse, but he shrugged and nodded.

'We'll have to make an early start if we're going to manage all of them,' Gil said, obviously delighted with the plan.

'Lovely; well, that's sorted. Isaac will appreciate that,' Molly said with a satisfied sigh.

Jenna smiled to herself, wondering if Joss Maitland realized what a very clever mother he had.

13

Molly looked up and smiled when Jenna joined her at the breakfast table next morning. 'The boys send their apologies,' she said. 'They left early to avoid the traffic jams. It can be gridlock on the motorway at this time of day.'

Jenna felt a stab of disappointment that she'd missed Gil. He'd been staying at Fenfleet since she arrived, and she'd half expected a knock on her bedroom door last night, but it never came. They'd hardly exchanged a word since Victoria's dramatic appearance — and he still had some explaining to do.

'You young people,' Molly tutted as Jenna declined Maria's offer of a cooked breakfast.

'It's fine,' Jenna assured her. 'I'm really not very hungry today.'

Molly's eyes slid to Gil's empty chair.

'You know best, dear,' she murmured.

It was nine-thirty when they drove through the gates of Fenfleet, and most of the early-morning haze had lifted as they set off at a leisurely pace for York. On getting up, Jenna had been reminded of Cornwall when she went to her bedroom window and saw the mist clinging to the trees, obscuring the furthest corners of the garden. She'd peered into the smoky haze, remembering boats clinking at their moorings in the St Ives harbour, and felt a sudden pang of nostalgia for the place. She had happy memories of Cornwall, and now they all came rushing back. There was her chance meeting with Gil in Truro, and then their trip to Polperro, with all the emotions that had stirred. She turned away from the window, her eyes moist, remembering Gil's first kiss as they'd watched the sun setting over Marazion beach.

The ring road was much quieter than it had been the previous evening when she drove back from the hospital with

Joss. Molly's little red BMW felt cosily comfortable as they headed into the city centre.

'I'll drop you off in town, Jenna,' she said, slowing for the lights at a busy junction.

Jenna glanced at her in surprise. She'd assumed Molly would want some company during her long day at the hospital.

'You didn't think I was going to subject you to hours by a hospital bedside trying to make conversation with two old-timers like us?' Her eyebrows had gone up as though to reprimand Jenna for her poor judgment. 'No, you'll have a much better time wandering through all the lovely shops. You should spoil yourself . . . buy a glamorous new outfit to stun us all at dinner.'

Jenna glanced down at the cream linen slacks and matching silk blouse she was wearing. They were the clothes she'd travelled in from Cornwall. She could feel herself smiling at the thought of a shopping spree.

Molly spotted the grin, and said, 'You see, I knew that would appeal to you. And we can round it off by meeting up for a bite of lunch later.'

She had it all thought out. Jenna found herself thinking that Molly Maitland was quite a woman. 'Well, if you're sure you don't mind,' she said.

Molly had pulled into the side of the road beside the historic city walls. 'There's a hotel just opposite the Minster,' she said. 'I'll see you in there at two o'clock.'

Jenna got out, and stood watching the car edge its way back into the stream of traffic. The mention of York Minster had sent a warm glow surging through her body. Every second of her time with Gil was etched into her heart. She walked slowly into town, entranced as ever by the old black-and-white timbered buildings leaning in higgledy-piggledy fashion against each other for support. She was soon in the busiest section, where the high-street chain

stores outnumbered the specialist boutiques. The only difference here was
that they occupied sites within the city's
old buildings, as did their own department store. Jenna paused when she
reached it, staring at the Maitland
name. The elegant dark green lettering
had been her idea. It was impossible
not to feel proud.

She wandered on, enjoying the bustle
of the crowds, before turning down to
the river, where she strolled along the
bank, pausing to admire the narrow
boats tied up alongside. One of them
had flowerpots lining its deck, while its
neighbour displayed an old bicycle
propped up against its cabin. She
smiled. York was a city of cyclists, but
she suspected this particular model had
been placed there for effect, for it
certainly didn't look roadworthy.

Finding a bench, she settled to watch
the river traffic. An image flashed into
her mind of the St Ives coastline rushing past as she and Gil skimmed over
the waves in his family's blue-and-white

launch. She closed her eyes, and she was back in their cove, the strength of Gil's arms around her. But another, less welcome, image was creeping into her head — that of a tall, wispy blonde kissing Gil. It was obvious she hadn't wanted him to know about her relationship with the enigmatic Mr Pemberley-Jones. Would Gil be jealous? Would he even care? Jenna doubted it. But, after the previous evening's performance, she was sure they hadn't seen the last of Victoria Symington.

Her thoughts of Cornwall made her think about Joss, and she wondered for the umpteenth time if he would go back. Maybe this was where he needed to be — here in Yorkshire, with the people who loved him — before he made any decisions about his future.

A cloud drifted across the sun, casting the river into shadow. Joss wasn't the only one facing difficult choices. Jenna knew she would have to return to London at some point, but she didn't want to think about that today. How could she face going back to a life without Gil? Maybe that was what Victoria was waiting for. Could Gil really end up with a woman like that? An icy chill ran through her veins, and she shivered. If she went home without having put up a fight for the man she loved, then he might well turn to Victoria — or someone very like her. The sun had emerged from behind its cloud again as she stood up, and began to stride purposefully towards the shops.

It was two hours later, laden with shiny carrier bags bearing the names of York's most expensive boutiques, when Jenna headed for her rendezvous with her aunt.

Molly was in the bar nursing a glass of red wine when she arrived, and she signalled the barman to pour another for her guest. Raising an appreciative eyebrow at Jenna's purchases, she said, 'I see you've taken my advice.'

Jenna chewed her lip and shot Molly a mischievous grin. 'I think I went a bit over the top.' She was remembering the slinky little red dress she'd bought, knowing it would hardly be suitable for dinner at Fenfleet. But, on the other hand . . . why not?

A waiter arrived and showed them to their table in a dining conservatory. A bank of lush green ferns and ivies, trailing from hanging baskets, gave the room a pleasant, musky atmosphere.

'I had to tell them we only wanted a snack, otherwise we couldn't have got a table so late in the day,' Molly explained, running her eye down the menu. 'Actually, the crab cakes are rather good here. I think I'll have those with some salad.'

Jenna nodded. 'I'll have the same, thank you,' she told the waiter, arranging her collection of bags so they wouldn't present a hazard to passing staff.

'How was Isaac today?' she asked, but she could tell from the older woman's sparkling eyes and general demeanour that the news was good.

'Very much better. Francine popped in for an hour after she dropped the twins off at nursery. That cheered Isaac up no end. In fact, he's been in such top form that he was complaining about being kept in bed.'

Jenna well knew her Uncle Isaac's stubborn streak. It was hard to dissuade him from a plan once his mind was made up. She smiled. 'That sounds encouraging.'

'Yes, it does, doesn't it?' Molly said thoughtfully. 'Of course, the difficult part now will be convincing him that he must stay in hospital until his doctors decide otherwise.'

'But if he really is so much improved, then maybe he could still rest at home?'

Molly wrinkled her nose. 'Perhaps . . . but, as you know, my dear, Isaac is not very good at taking a back seat. But he'll have to hand over the reins to Gil at some point. Besides,' she shrugged, 'it's not as though he wasn't more or less running the business on his own anyway.'

'Wait a minute . . . you say Gil is going to run the company?'

Molly put up her hands and shrugged. 'Well, Joss doesn't seem to want it. I'm not sure Gil is all that comfortable about it either, but we don't want it falling into the hands of strangers.'

'We don't know for sure that Joss won't agree to take over.' Jenna bit her lip, considering. She was remembering their conversation in the car yesterday when he'd suggested she might play a part in the business. 'Maybe there's another way,' she said, quietly. 'Let me think about it.'

Molly's eyes narrowed. 'What are you up to, Jenna?'

'Nothing . . . really . . . at least, nothing worth mentioning yet.'

But Molly's sharp mind was racing ahead. 'You think there might be a chance Joss will stay?'

Jenna shrugged. 'I don't think even Joss knows that yet. But I can tell you that the reason he was in Cornwall was to paint.'

Molly nodded. 'He's made that very plain.'

'No, I mean *really* paint. You should see how many canvases he's completed down there. I don't think he ever slept.' She glanced up at her aunt's rapt face. 'The thing is, Molly, Joss is a great painter. I think his work is good enough to exhibit.'

'Really?' Molly stared at Jenna, amazed. She tilted her head to study her in a way that reminded her of Joss. 'You really think he's that good?'

'I'd say so, but I'd want Dad to have a look at his canvases.'

'Well, we will have to see what Daniel says when he gets here tomorrow,' Molly said.

Jenna stared at her in astonishment. 'My father's coming to Yorkshire? But he never said . . . '

'You know Daniel better than any of us. He's not given to doing the expected.'

Jenna frowned, but the arrival of their meals prevented further discussion, and as the appetizing smell of the crab cakes reached her she realized she was actually hungry.

'Delicious,' she said ten minutes later, laying her cutlery at the side of her empty plate. 'Are we going back to the hospital now?'

Molly glanced at her watch. 'The ward sister insists on her patients having an hour's nap in the afternoon, so they don't allow visitors in until four o'clock. And Gil and Joss should be there by then.'

Jenna's heart gave its familiar lurch at the mention of Gil's name.

'So there's no hurry for us to get back.' Molly settled back in her chair. 'Tell me some more about what sort of things my son paints.'

Jenna couldn't hide her surprise. 'You must have seen some samples of his work.'

Molly's eyes narrowed. 'Not a single thing. Oh, I know he was sketching and maybe doing bits of painting at Fenfleet, but he was very protective of all that. He never showed any of them to Isaac or myself.'

Jenna remembered how reluctant Joss had been to show her any of his canvases in St Ives. But not to allow his parents to see his talents . . . She sat back, shocked. 'You've really never seen Joss's work?'

Molly shook her head and looked so sad that Jenna reached across to touch her arm. 'Perhaps he just doesn't realize how interested you are.' She paused to consider how to word what she was going to say next. In the end, she just said it. 'I suspect Joss is quite insecure. He doesn't trust himself . . . doesn't believe he has this wonderful talent.' She glanced up at Molly. 'If it's any consolation, he doesn't show his work to anyone. I think he's frightened they'll tell him it's no good. It's such a shame because his paintings are wonderful.'

Her brows knitted before she went on. 'Actually, I've been wondering if this is the real reason why he doesn't want to get involved in the business. Maybe Joss is simply terrified of failure.'

Her aunt frowned and her hand went up to dismiss the idea, but Jenna carried on. 'Let's consider this from his point of view. He's seen you and Isaac develop the business into the success it is today. And now you've taken Gil into the company — a man who has the same flair for business as you and Isaac. Where does that leave Joss? What if he deliberately went in a different direction, concentrated on his painting, just so he didn't have to prove himself in the business?'

Molly was stunned. 'Joss has nothing to prove,' she said.

'We both know that, but I'm talking about Joss.'

For a few moments Molly was silent, then she fixed Jenna with a questioning stare. 'You really think this could be the case?'

Jenna swallowed. 'I don't know. It's possible. Obviously, no one would want to force him into doing something he was violently opposed to. But if it really is a confidence thing, then maybe some kind of trial run could be set up — something that would give him a taste of what it's like running the business, but without the pressure. I'm sure Gil might have an idea of how to go about it.'

Molly was thoughtful. 'It's certainly worth considering. And if you're right, Jenna . . . ' Her eyes lit up. 'Well, if you're right — we might just get our son back.'

The sight of Gil's car as they drove onto the hospital site later that afternoon sent Jenna's heart into an alarming flip. But she wasn't so absorbed in the thrill of seeing him again as not to notice the new spring in Molly's step. Whether that was down to her husband's improvement or their earlier discussion about Joss, Jenna had no idea. She thought it was probably a bit of both.

Isaac Maitland had lost his pale, pinched look of yesterday. He was sitting up in bed, in animated conversation with Joss and Gil when Jenna and

Molly walked into the room. Gil's eyes went immediately to Jenna, sending ripples of pleasure through her. She gave him a wide smile and nodded a greeting to the others.

'Darling.' Isaac Maitland smiled, holding his arms wide to his wife. 'And you've brought young Jenna back with you.'

Gil and Joss sprang to their feet, vacating their chairs for the two women. Jenna was aware of Gil standing behind her. Once during the visit, when she spoke to answer a question from Isaac, Gil bent close to catch her words, and she caught the faint smell of his aftershave. The conversation centred on the day's whistle-stop trip to the Leeds, Harrogate and York stores. Surprisingly, Joss seemed to be doing most of the talking.

Isaac Maitland was displaying a delighted grin. 'What was your real opinion of the stores, son? You'll have noticed we've kept ourselves busy while you were away.'

Jenna saw Joss wince, but there was

no confrontation in his blue eyes. 'If you're talking about the expansion of the Harrogate shop, then yes, I noticed that had started. You and Gil run a tight ship, Dad.'

'So, you don't think we can make any improvements, then?' Isaac's shrewd eyes were studying his son.

'There's always room for improvement, Dad.'

Isaac Maitland raised an eyebrow, and Gil said, 'Joss has been highlighting some new markets for us.'

'Really?' He shot a glance at his wife. 'Do go on.'

'Well, for a start,' Joss said, 'you don't sell artists' materials in any of the stores.'

A smile went round the room, but Joss was getting into his stride. 'I'm serious. So many people paint now. You only have to look at all the art groups and societies springing up around the country. We could start small by just stocking a few basic kits. They wouldn't take up much space.'

Jenna wondered if the others noticed

he'd said 'we'. She picked up on his idea. 'Why not go all the way and dedicate some space in the stores to create art galleries . . . or use the work of local artists in the restaurants and coffee shops? That way we are encouraging new talent, and the company benefits from a percentage of the sale.'

Joss's eyes were shining. 'What a great idea, Jenna.' He grinned at her. 'I said you were good at this.'

Gil's hand was on her shoulder. She could feel the warmth of it through her thin blouse, and her senses tingled. 'Joss came up with another idea today,' he said.

'That's right,' said Joss. 'I think we could make more of being right here in Yorkshire.'

His father looked puzzled, so he went on, 'We could sell experiences . . . walking excursions linked to bed-and-breakfast accommodation . . . pony trekking . . . car racing . . . even trips in hot air balloons, if that's what the public want.'

Isaac Maitland frowned. 'Doesn't the

tourist board already have all that covered?'

Joss nodded, his face glowing. He was clearly enjoying himself. 'And I'm sure they would welcome our involvement. They would still put the leisure packages together, but we could sell the idea to our customers in-store for a small commission.'

'He could be right,' Gil said. 'It might not make us a fortune, but if we promote it properly it could be great for customer relations.'

Jenna caught Molly's glance and smiled. Isaac was beaming at his son. His day had obviously been a success.

The conversation turned to the prospect of Isaac's homecoming, which didn't look to Jenna as if it would be too far off. When visiting time was almost up, she suggested waiting outside again to give Isaac and Molly a few moments of privacy before the end of the visit.

'How's your day been, Jenna?' Joss asked as they waited in the corridor outside.

She knew Gil had been watching her and wondered why he suddenly seemed uneasy. Had something happened that neither of them had mentioned? But she turned to Joss and gave him a dazzling smile. 'Wonderful,' she said. 'Molly dropped me off in town before coming to visit your dad. I hit the shops and spent a fortune.'

'Every penny well spent,' Molly laughed as she joined them. 'And doesn't Isaac look well?' Her eyes were shining and she looked relaxed. What a difference a day had made.

Everyone nodded and Joss and Jenna shared a grin. Only Gil looked worried — and then they all knew why.

He cleared his throat and took a deep breath. 'I've been putting off mentioning it, Molly — ' He forced a smile, but it came out like an apologetic grimace. 'Victoria's invited herself to dinner tonight.'

They all stared at him, and then Joss chuckled. 'Good old Vicky; she was never slow at coming forward.'

But Molly was annoyed. 'The little madam,' she hissed.

Gil spread his arms. 'She says she has a gift for Isaac and she'll call round at dinner tonight. I certainly didn't invite her.'

Molly gave an exasperated sigh. 'I've a good mind to turn her away.'

Jenna tried to swallow her disappointment. Everything was spoiled. The evening she had been so looking forward to — the evening when Gil would have eyes only for her — was to be Victoria's triumph instead of Jenna's. She felt sick as they made their way to the cars.

When they reached the car park, Molly once again announced she would drive back with Gil, leaving Joss and Jenna to follow in her BMW. Jenna saw Gil's frown, and hoped it was because he'd wanted to drive her to Fenfleet himself. She gave him a smiling shrug. She knew Molly would want to ask Gil about Joss, and how the visits to the stores had really gone.

Joss was quiet as they joined the busy teatime traffic, but when Jenna glanced up at him, he was smiling. 'You really enjoyed yourself today, didn't you?' she said.

'Hmm . . . I did, actually,' he said slowly.

'You sound surprised.'

'Well, it was different.'

'Maybe it's you who is different, Joss. You came up with some really great ideas back there. Isaac thought so too, I could tell.'

14

'Molly tells me you've got some bags to be carried upstairs,' Gil said, coming forward as Joss pulled up at the front steps of the house.

Jenna could have managed the packages perfectly well on her own, but she wasn't about to pass up this chance of being alone with Gil. He collected the shiny bags from the boot of Molly's BMW and followed her upstairs to her room.

'At last.' He grinned, laying the bags on a cream wicker chair and crossing the floor to take Jenna in his arms. 'I've been looking forward to this all day,' he murmured as his lips brushed her hair, her face, her mouth.

In Gil's arms, she could forget the rest of the world. Her head was spinning, her body aflame. His kisses were hungry and she matched his passion, only pulling away reluctantly when her phone rang.

'Ignore it,' Gil whispered, his voice low. But she freed herself from his arms, laughing. 'It might be important.'

It had stopped ringing by the time she had rummaged in her bag, and when she checked the 'missed calls' facility she saw it had been her father. She put the phone on her bedside table, in no hurry to return his call.

Gil's gaze had never left her. 'I'm sorry about Victoria,' he said, spreading his hands in a gesture of helplessness. 'I had no idea she would turn up like that last night.'

Jenna threw him a rueful grin. 'Do you have this trouble with all your ex-girlfriends?'

His eyes clouded. 'She was never exactly a girlfriend. I told you. We only went out a couple of times, but it was enough for me to realize she was trouble. I've spent the rest of the time since then avoiding her.' He frowned. 'I can't imagine what she was doing in Cornwall, though. I suppose it was a spur of the moment thing. She somehow found out that Joss was going down there and asked to tag along.'

Jenna had been wondering if she should recount her earlier meeting with Victoria. She didn't owe the girl anything, so why not? 'There might be more to it than that,' she confided.

Gil's jaw dropped in astonishment when she told him of the encounter in the St Ives artist's bedroom. He whistled. 'So she had a man down there all along. Well, at least I can stop feeling sorry for her.'

When Gil left, Jenna picked up her phone and rang her father. 'But I must have mentioned to you that I was coming up to Yorkshire,' he protested.

'You really are incorrigible, Dad. You know perfectly well that you didn't tell me.'

She could hear him tutting at the other end. 'OK,' he conceded. 'I've been rumbled. I wanted to surprise you, but I suppose Molly let the cat out of the bag?'

Jenna suppressed a grin. 'You've surprised me, alright. When will you be arriving?'

'We're coming by train, so your guess

is as good as mine. Just expect me when you see me.'

It wasn't until he had signed off that she realized Daniel had said 'we'. Who was he bringing with him? she wondered, intrigued.

The day's purchases were still stacked where Gil had left them. She glanced at the shiny black bag, where the expensive red dress nestled in its layers of tissue. She'd abandoned the idea of wearing it when she realized Victoria would be there this evening. But why not? Why shouldn't she glam up? She could give Victoria Symington a run for her money any day.

After the dust of the busy York streets, the warm, foamy bath felt luxurious. Jenna lay back, eyes closed, enjoying the sensual pleasure of the delicately-perfumed essential oils she had added. The water felt silky on her skin as she went over the day's events. Her conversation with Molly had been exhilarating at the time; but now, with hindsight, she worried that she'd perhaps given her aunt false hopes that Joss might be persuaded to stay. And yet . . . She pursed her lips as she went over the conversation around Isaac's hospital bed. Joss had talked enthusiastically about the business — even suggested improvements, some of which were really good ideas. Would he have done that if he hadn't cared?

She paid special attention to her appearance that night. One final look in her bedroom mirror confirmed she'd been right to buy the gorgeous red dress. She felt good in it. Her freshly-washed hair was shining, and the new, darker shadow and mascara she'd bought made her eyes sparkle. Jenna felt on top of the world as she walked downstairs to join the others.

Gil's eyes widened and he mouthed a silent 'wow' as she entered the drawing room.

Her efforts hadn't been lost on Joss, either. 'You look knockout tonight, Jenna,' he said, glancing around the room at the others. 'You put the rest of us to shame.'

Jenna laughed. 'That's only because Francine hasn't yet arrived.'

'Well, I'm here now,' called a voice from the door, 'and Joss is right. That dress is amazing.' Francine threw her husband a mischievous scowl. 'Why can't I have one like that?'

He was about to tell her, when his mother appeared and suggested he should pour the ladies a drink. Jenna called her thanks and watched as the golden sherry filled the small crystal glasses. Joss handed one to her and she settled herself happily on the sofa next to Molly, aware that Gil still hadn't taken his eyes off her. The little red dress was having exactly the effect she had intended.

The blissful moment was shattered when the door flew open and Victoria sailed in. Her blonde hair had been piled up into some elaborate Grecian style. She went straight to Gil and threw her arms around him. Jenna stared uncomfortably at the carpet as Victoria kissed Gil's cheek. Her short black dress hugged her body like a second skin, and her silver sandals had five-inch heels. Jenna fought back the hope that she would teeter off them and fall flat on her exquisitely-made-up face.

'I suppose you'll want a drink, Victoria,' Molly sighed, signalling to Joss.

Apparently only just now realizing that Gil wasn't the only person in the room, Victoria swept over to Molly's side and took her hand, giving her version of a sympathetic smile. There was no evidence of the gift she'd allegedly brought for Isaac. 'And how is the poor man today?'

Jenna saw Molly's shoulders stiffen. 'The *poor man*, as you call him, is much improved, thank you,' she replied, stiffly, not bothering to hide her irritation at the young woman's patronising behaviour. 'In fact, we hope to have him home in a day or two.'

'Wonderful.' Victoria clapped her hands. 'Didn't I say everything would be just fine?'

She turned her bright smile on Joss,

switching her glance between him and Francine. 'You two patched things up then?'

Jenna heard Molly gasp, but the reopening of the drawing room door drowned out her comment.

'Dinner's all ready whenever you are,' Maria announced.

Victoria's chatter dominated the conversation around the dinner table, but they all looked up when she addressed Jenna.

'Didn't I see you in York today?'

Jenna nodded. 'Possibly. I was shopping in town. Can't say I noticed you, though.'

Victoria's eyebrow lifted just a fraction, and then she smiled, victory in her eyes. 'It was Guy who recognized you, actually. He was telling me about bumping into you the other day.' She spoke teasingly, as though there had been some kind of romantic tryst involved. Then she paused, enjoying the fact that she had everyone's attention. 'No lasting damage, I trust?'

All eyes went to Jenna, and she felt her colour rise.

'You never mentioned anything about meeting Guy Bradford,' Gil said.

'It was nothing. I'd forgotten all about it.' The man had tried to imply there was still a relationship between Gil and Victoria. He'd been making mischief; just as he'd tried to upset Francine by suggesting Joss had run off to Cornwall with another woman. Neither of his allegations was true, so what would have been the point of antagonizing Gil with the story? But now she had no option but to relate their meeting. She told them about the bicycle incident, and the subsequent drink she and Guy had shared in the village pub. 'He said he knew all of you; dropped me back at the house, in fact,' she said, her chin lifting defensively. 'I didn't realize he was a close family friend, or I would have mentioned that we'd met.'

Joss was frowning. 'The man's a rogue — and not even a likeable one.'

'Guy's nothing of the kind.' Victoria's voice rose indignantly. 'Tell them, Gil . . . He's your friend, after all.'

Gil's expression was cold, his eyes still on Jenna. 'You should have mentioned you'd met him,' he repeated icily.

Jenna bit her lip as an uncomfortable silence filled the room. Victoria suddenly jumped up. 'Goodness, is that the time? I know it's shocking manners, Molly, but we've almost finished dinner. The thing is . . . I've promised to meet someone in ten minutes.' She left the table and looked back at Gil. 'Will you give me a lift, darling?'

They all stared at her. 'I'll call a taxi,' Gil said, coldly.

'But I'll be late,' she bleated.

Jenna fought to control her fury. This woman was outrageous! She'd joined their table without being invited, and dominated every conversation. She'd spent the entire evening upsetting everyone. It was more than Jenna could bear.

'Oh, for heaven's sake, Gil, just take

her out of here,' she snapped. Her fingers itched to slap the woman.

Gil's eyes blazed with anger as he strode ahead of Victoria to the door. Jenna wasn't sure if his rage was directed at her or their uninvited guest. She knew everyone was looking at her, their eyes questioning, but she'd had enough. She excused herself and fled to her room. Francine's worried voice trailed after her: 'Are you alright, Jenna?'

'I'm fine,' she lied. 'Just a bit of a headache. I'm going to have an early night.'

It was forty minutes before the quiet tap came at her door. Thinking it was Gil, she steeled herself for what she was sure would be some kind of confrontation. But it was Joss who stood, serious-faced, on the landing.

'We've upset you, Jenna,' he said quietly. 'Gil should never have spoken to you like that, and Victoria was just making mischief. Who cares if you met Guy Bradford? We certainly don't.'

Jenna sighed but managed a smile. 'I'll have to think about going home soon.' She fidgeted with the door handle. 'I doubt very much if Gil wants me to stay now anyway,' she said, quietly.

'Gil doesn't know what's good for him,' Joss said.

'Has he come back yet?' Jenna asked, still harbouring a tinge of disappointment that it had been Joss who knocked at her door and not Gil.

He glanced away, uneasily. 'No, not yet.'

Jenna's heart sank. She had no doubt at all that Victoria would be making the most of her time alone with Gil.

She met Joss's eyes. 'My father will be arriving tomorrow ... and I've decided to go back with him when he leaves.'

She saw the surprise in her cousin's eyes, but he knew this wasn't the time for protests. 'We can talk about this later,' he said quietly as he turned away.

The house was quiet as Jenna

undressed mechanically and got into bed. Lying in the darkness she went over her day. Why was she giving in to this wilful girl? Could she really just give up on Gil and run away? She fell into a fitful sleep.

In her dream, there was a light in the outside corridor, and when a shadow fell across the lighted gap at the bottom of her door, she saw herself getting out of bed to investigate. She held her breath. Someone was standing there! Her heart was thudding . . . it could only be Gil! The door wasn't locked. All he had to do was turn the handle. She waited, not daring to breathe, willing him to open it. She closed her eyes. In her mind she saw him silently cross the thick bedroom carpet, a look of longing in his eyes as he reached out for her. But the door didn't open. Jenna saw herself shivering in her thin nightdress. She heard the soft sound of feet shifting — and the shadow moved away. The tears she had been fighting all day suddenly spilled over, and she had neither the will nor the energy to stop them.

Her pillow was still wet when she woke up next morning, and the day outside looked as bleak and grey as she felt. She was dreading going downstairs to face the family after her unexpectedly dramatic exit after dinner last night. But, to her relief, she was first down. She wandered out into the garden. It was one of those mornings after a night of rain when everything still dripped. There were beads of moisture on the pink roses and their dark leaves glistened. She took a deep breath, feeling the moist air hit the back of her throat.

She hadn't heard Joss come into the garden. His expression was grim.

'What's happened?' she cried. 'It's not Isaac, is it?'

He shook his head. 'It's Gil. He didn't come back last night. No reason why he should come here, of course, because he has his own place in the next village, but . . . '

Jenna's heart sank. Joss was trying to break it to her gently that Gil had spent the night with Victoria. What other explanation could there be? Her hand clutched her throat. It was she who'd sent him off with her.

Joss touched her shoulder. 'Maybe I shouldn't have told you, but Francine and I could see you and Gil were getting close. We both felt you ought to know.'

Jenna opened her mouth to speak, but no words came. Her world was in pieces.

'There's a full coffee pot at the bungalow if you don't fancy facing the rest of us this morning,' he said. 'And Francine is a great listener.'

Jenna sighed. Less than a week ago, she had been the one listening to Francine's problems. Now the situation was reversed. She nodded. 'Thanks, Joss. Will you make my excuses to Molly?'

Walking through the garden reminded her of Gil — but then everything reminded her of Gil. She should have handled things better last evening, but instead she'd sent him into another woman's arms. She had only herself to blame for whatever happened last night.

'You're not really going back to London with Daniel, are you?' Francine asked as she poured Jenna a mug of steaming coffee. The au pair she'd yet to meet was getting the children dressed in another room while the two women talked.

Jenna shrugged. 'I don't see any point in staying on here, not now that Isaac is on the mend — and you and Joss seem to be sorting things out.'

'There was never anything really wrong between Joss and me.' Francine shrugged, cradling the bright yellow coffee mug. 'Well, not seriously. He just doesn't want to be pitched into running the business. He'd much rather be down in Cornwall, painting.'

'Why don't you go back to St Ives with him, Francine . . . and take the children with you? If he really doesn't want to be part of the Maitland empire, you could all still have a good life down there.'

Francine put down her coffee. 'Don't think it hasn't been discussed. We've talked about these things long into the night. The talking part is easy, it's the deciding that is so difficult.'

'Oh, I don't know. Some decisions get made for you,' Jenna said. She sounded so sad and lost that Francine reached across the table for her hand.

'You were the one telling me to talk to Joss . . . remember, Jenna?' She tapped the table. 'Right here in this kitchen, you told me that things were not always what they seemed. And you were right. Joss hadn't gone off with another woman. Deep down I knew that.' She squeezed Jenna's hand. 'Sometimes you just have to trust people.'

But tears blurred Jenna's vision as she slowly shook her head. 'I sent Gil away with Victoria,' she sniffed. 'And he stayed out all night with her. Where's the trust in that?'

'I don't know the answer to that. But

I do know Gil owes you an explanation. Why don't you go over to his cottage and talk to him?'

But Jenna shook her head. The humiliation of finding Victoria still with him would be more than she could bear.

Francine got up and went to pluck a set of car keys from a row of hooks by the back door. She put them on the table in front of Jenna. 'It's the blue Mini in the garage,' she said, patting Jenna's shoulder. 'Go and see Gil.'

15

Jenna rested her head against the black leather driving seat of Francine's Mini. She desperately wanted to see Gil again, but if he really had spent the night with Victoria, she could be making the biggest mistake of her life. There was nothing to stop her from going right now to pack her bags. She closed her eyes, trying not to think about what she would be leaving behind. Less than two weeks ago she had never even heard of Gil Maitland . . . only two short weeks . . . and now her life had been turned upside down.

Images of York's ancient cobbled streets, red-pantiled roofs and higgledy-piggledy black-and-white timbered buildings flooded into her mind. She was back up amongst the gargoyles of York Minster. She was with Gil — and he was kissing her! She was blinking back a blur of tears. She would go to him. All she had to do was to turn on this car's ignition . . .

Jenna remembered Oak Tree Cottage from the number of times she had cycled past during her early years at Fenfleet. But in those days the garden had been overgrown, and green paint peeling from the door and windows. It all looked very different now. The straggly garden had been replaced with a neatly-cropped lawn, and the colourful flower borders were orderly. Purple clematis scrambled over the front porch, where the door had a fresh coat of white paint. Gil's green sports car was parked in the drive.

Jenna had a sudden urge to drive on. Coming here had been a foolish idea. Just as she'd decided not to stop, the front door opened and Gil stepped out. Jenna gasped. There was an angry dark bruise beneath his left eye.

He hadn't recognized Francine's car, and turned as Jenna pulled up at the gate. She stopped and got out and walked towards him.

His embarrassment at seeing her like this was obvious. He ran his hand through his hair and looked away. She should turn and go, but that would make her look even more foolish than she was already feeling. She kept her voice light. 'Been in the wars?' she asked.

Gil's fingers went to his bruise. 'I bumped into the door,' he muttered.

Jenna's eyes narrowed. 'Really,' she said. 'It looks like you bumped into someone's fist. Jealous boyfriend, was it?'

'What! You think . . . Oh, I see . . . you think the man Victoria was meeting last night did this?'

Jenna shrugged and lifted her chin, defiantly. 'I don't much care who caused it. You probably deserved it.'

'Right!' Gil grabbed her hand and marched her into the cottage. They were in a bright yellow kitchen where copper pans gleamed on an open shelf. 'Sit down,' he ordered, indicating one of four kitchen chairs, 'and I'll tell you what happened.'

Jenna waited, not sure she wanted to hear what was coming.

'It was Guy Bradford she was meeting . . . at the same pub where he took you. But we were late in arriving and he was just leaving. He recognized my car, and before Victoria had even got out he was striding across the car park, yelling at us.

'Victoria got out and tried to calm him down. He'd been drinking, of course, and had got the wrong end of the stick. He was throwing his arms about, accusing us of having an affair.

'I got out of the car and tried to restrain him.' He met Jenna's eyes. 'I didn't use force . . . honestly. I just grabbed his collar. His arms were flailing about and he caught himself on the eye.

'Victoria came at me like a wildcat, screaming that I had attacked Guy. Her handbag caught the side of my face . . . ' He touched his bruise. 'It looked much worse last night, which is why I thought it best to come home and spend the night in the cottage. I was on my way to Fenfleet to explain . . . ' His hands went out in a helpless gesture.

It was the most preposterous story Jenna had ever heard, and just ridiculous enough to be true. She put up her hand to hide her grin. 'You were floored by a woman's handbag?'

He sighed. 'I know. I'm not surprised if you don't believe it. I should just have told you I got this defending a lady's honour. You would have accepted that, even if you never spoke to me again.

'To be honest, Jenna . . . ' He took her hand. The dark eyes held hers and their power over her was as potent as ever. She could feel her knees tremble. ' . . . I was so mad at the pair of them that I needed to calm down. It didn't occur to me until this morning what you all must have been thinking when I didn't go back to Fenfleet last night.'

His eyes were still exploring hers. 'What did you think had happened?' he asked quietly.

Jenna felt the heat rush to her cheeks and she looked away. But he touched her face and gently turned it towards him again. 'You thought I had spent the night with Victoria, didn't you?'

She was on the verge of tears. 'I didn't know what to think. She'd been making a play for you all night, and had annoyed me so much that all I wanted was to get rid of her.' She swallowed. 'Honestly, Gil, I could see my hands round her throat if she stayed at Fenfleet a second longer. That's why I told you to take her away. I didn't much care where. I just wanted her out of my sight.'

He smiled grimly. 'Let's hope we have finally achieved that.'

Jenna raised an eyebrow and Gil went on, 'The last I saw of them, Guy was splayed across the pub car park looking very sorry for himself, and Victoria was cradling his head and cooing words of comfort into his ear. They're a well-matched pair.'

Suddenly, Jenna couldn't keep a

straight face. 'Pity you didn't have a camera with you. You could have made a fortune from a picture like that.'

Gil touched his bruised cheek and winced. 'That pair deserve each other. Let's hope they stay together now, and leave the rest of us alone.'

He held out his arms and Jenna went into them. 'I thought I'd lost you, Gil.' Her voice was trembling. 'I came here to tell you we were finished, that I never wanted to see you again.'

His hand cradled her head, his fingers stroking the soft silkiness of her hair. 'Don't ever say that, Jenna.' He touched her chin, lifting it until he could see the tears sparkling in her eyes. His voice was gentle. 'I don't think I could live without you now.'

Jenna's eyes closed as his mouth came down on hers.

16

It was early afternoon before they left Gil's cottage, convoying in both cars back to Fenfleet so Jenna could return Francine's Mini.

'They've all gone to the hospital,' Esme informed Jenna when she asked after the family. 'Shouldn't think they'll be back before five.'

Jenna nodded her thanks and hurried back to Gil. He was leaning, arms folded, against his car, watching Jenna as she ran down the front steps to join him. 'I like it when you smile like that,' she teased.

He cupped a finger under her chin, tipping it up to kiss her softly on the mouth. 'I've got something to smile about now,' he said, looking deep into her eyes.

They were no longer strangers, but he still had the power to make her skin tingle and her cheeks glow.

'Have I told you recently how beautiful you are, Miss Maitland?'

She smiled and raised his fingers to her lips.

'And that I love you. Did I mention that?'

'Over and over again,' Jenna laughed.

The lines around Gil's face tightened and she could see the depth of feeling in his eyes. 'Good,' he said. 'I don't want you to be in any doubt about that.'

She was still up in the clouds an hour later as they drove through the electronic gate and into the staff car park of the Maitlands' York store. Outside, the busy city streets were still bustling, and in the distance the Minster bells were tolling out three o'clock. In the elevator, he lifted her hand to kiss it. 'I won't be long in the office,' he promised. 'But I must get these letters off today. And there are a couple of important business calls that can't wait.'

Jenna assured him she didn't mind. She was looking forward to familiarizing herself with the store again. 'I'll have a good old wander around,' she said, her eyes sparkling. 'It will be just like old times.'

She started her nostalgic tour in the leisure department. It had been given a smart new look since her day, but she could still see many other possibilities for improvement. Her brain was already whirring, working out ways to attract even more customers to this floor. Joss's art idea, and a gallery to display the work of local artists, would be perfect for here. She wondered if anyone had considered offering it as a franchise.

She was in Ladies' Fashions when Jane Harper appeared at her elbow with a smile. 'Mr Ryder thought you might like some company.'

The two women strolled through the department together, with Jane pointing out the new lines and explaining the new staff benefits. She said, 'It was Mr Gil's idea to set up an employees' shares scheme, so that technically everyone owns a tiny part of the business. If the stores prosper, then so do the employees. It's made everyone even more committed to the stores' success.'

Jenna remembered how much the feeling of community spirit amongst the staff had impressed her when she came here with Gil a few days ago. 'What a great idea,' she said.

Miss Harper nodded, and there was a glint of pride in her eye. 'Yes,' she said quietly. 'We all thought so.'

It was another thirty minutes before Gil appeared at her side. He nodded his thanks to Miss Harper, who glanced at her watch and hurried off, excusing herself.

'So, how was the trip down Memory Lane?' He grinned down at her.

She hardly needed to answer. He could tell by the charge of excitement in her eyes that she'd been reliving old times. She glanced around, savouring the hum of the busy store. 'I'd forgotten how much I enjoyed it all.'

'You could come back, you know. Isaac and Molly would love that.'

She met his eyes. 'And what about you, Gil? Would you love it if I came back?'

The muscles in his jaw tightened as he gazed down at her. 'What do you think?'

She was quiet on the short drive to the hospital. Her head was buzzing with plans, ideas for improvements. She had to remind herself that the running of the store was no longer any of her business. She had forfeited that two years ago. She sighed. It still didn't stop the adrenalin buzz when she walked the shop floor.

She didn't notice Gil glancing down at her. He said nothing, but he could tell by her face how fired up she was. There was a new eagerness in her eyes that made him suspect Joss had been right all along, and that Jenna was itching to take up the company reins again. He pursed his lips . . . thinking.

But he knew she was too devoted a daughter to ever leave her father.

'You missed Daniel,' Isaac announced when Jenna and Gil walked into his hospital room. 'The old rogue sat on my bed and ate all my grapes.' But there was a twinkle in his eye. There might have been bad blood between the brothers when Daniel turned his back on the business, leaving Molly and Isaac to build up the family empire on their own, but all that was water under the bridge now.

Jenna moved forward and kissed Isaac's cheek. 'Did you two have a good visit?'

Isaac threw a rueful grin in Molly's direction. 'It was alright . . . I suppose.'

Tessa sensed an air of conspiracy, for she hadn't missed the knowing glances that passed between Joss and Francine.

'Where is Dad now?' she asked.

'He took a taxi back to Fenfleet,' Molly replied. 'He said something about wanting to rest and clean up before the evening meal.'

Jenna frowned. Resting and cleaning

up didn't sound like the dad she knew. Daniel Maitland thrived on perpetual energy — and as for cleaning up . . . She thought of the crumpled jacket and paint-splashed jeans that were his usual attire. 'Is Dad alright?'

The four Maitlands smiled in unison. 'He's just fine, Jenna, dear. You'll see,' Molly said.

They were definitely up to something. And, from the mischievous expression on Isaac's face, he was in on it.

She scowled as she sat next to Gil on the way back to Fenfleet. 'I don't suppose you know what's going on?' She glanced at his handsome profile and her eyes narrowed.

Gil shrugged. 'I'm as intrigued as you. And the answer is: no, I haven't a clue what they're up to, but I agree . . . something is definitely going on.'

The family had gathered in the drawing room, each nursing a drink, when Jenna and Gil joined them. There was still no sign of her dad.

'Daniel will be down directly,' Molly

said, answering Jenna's unasked question.

Joss poured drinks for the new arrivals, and they all stood around with an air of expectancy.

Then a voice from the door said, 'I see you've started without me.'

Jenna swung round. 'Dad!' She ran forward to hug him. That was when she noticed he was wearing a new cream linen suit. His blue patterned shirt was open at the neck and a turquoise kerchief was knotted at his throat. She stepped back to take in the new attire. 'My, don't you look the dandy.'

He made a twirl and threw up a hand in a final flourish. 'I thought I'd better make the effort. It is a special occasion after all.'

Jenna stared at him, then her suspicious glance covered the room. 'How can you all know when we haven't told anyone yet?'

She held out her hand to Gil and he crossed the floor to put an arm around her.

'I've asked Jenna to marry me.' His eyes twinkled with tenderness as he gazed down at her. 'And she's accepted.' He turned to Daniel. 'So, with your permission, sir . . . we are engaged.'

Eyebrows shot up around the room. Molly clapped her hands. 'But that's wonderful news!' she laughed.

Francine and Joss came forward to embrace Jenna and shake Gil's hand.

Only Daniel hung back, and Jenna though she'd seen a glint of tears in his eyes. Then he threw his arms wide and she ran to him. 'So my little girl is getting married.'

'I thought you had all guessed.'

Joss stepped forward, holding Francine's hand. 'We had our suspicions,' he teased. 'And it's wonderful. It certainly trumps my news.'

'What news is that, Joss?' Jenna asked.

Joss bit his lip, studying the floor, choosing his words carefully. 'We've all had a chat about this at the hospital, and everyone is in agreement.'

Jenna held her breath.

'I'm not going back to Cornwall.' He put up a hand before she could speak. 'It doesn't mean I'm going to give up my painting. I'm not prepared to do that. But I've been talking with Daniel, and he has agreed to set up an exhibition for me at the gallery — if he thinks my canvases are good enough, of course.'

Jenna grinned. 'They're good enough, Joss. You know they are.'

He took a deep breath. 'I'm not promising anything, but I will have another go at the business. I still don't harbour any ambitions of taking over the company, but I will do my best to be a part of it.'

He turned to Jenna. 'And that's where you come in, Jenna.'

Jenna stared at him, her eyes wide. 'I don't understand. What does it have to do with me?'

'Well, me doing my little bit won't be enough. Dad needs to have someone he can trust to get involved in the business full-time.' He met Jenna's eyes and smiled. 'Someone with your commit-ment, Jenna, your fire and determination. I put all those emotions into my paint-ing, but your passion is the Maitland family business. We can all see it. We need you, Jenna.'

Jenna threw a beseeching look at Gil and he gave her an understanding smile. But the decision was hers to make.

She bit her lip. 'I have a job.' She looked at her father. 'Dad needs me to run the gallery.'

She waited for Daniel to back her up, confirm she was indispensable, but he waved his hand. 'Claire can do all that. You've trained her well, Jenna.' He glanced around the room. 'We've all talked about this. It's time for you to think of yourself, to do what you really want.' He smiled, and his ruggedly handsome face lit up. 'Never think I don't appreciate everything you've done for me. I know how much you would rather have stayed on in Yorkshire, following in Isaac's footsteps. You didn't have to give it all up to come to London and help me, but you did ... and because of that, I still have my gallery.'

'You don't have to say this, Dad. Gil and I have talked about it, and we're not going to get married straight away. I've no intention of leaving you on your own.'

Daniel's chin lifted and his blue eyes twinkled. 'What makes you think I'd be on my own?'

Jenna's mouth dropped open.

'There's someone I want you to meet. She's just in the next room.' He went out, and they heard him take long strides across the hall. When he came back, he was holding a woman's hand.

'Caroline!' Gil gasped. 'What are you doing here?'

Gil's sister smiled, a little hesitantly. 'Daniel and I have been seeing quite a bit of each other.'

Jenna's father threw her a good-natured grimace. 'Don't look so shocked, daughter. It was your fault we got together in the first place.' He nodded to Gil. 'Well, both of yours, I suppose.'

Gil gave Jenna a bewildered shrug.

'It was that picture you bought for Caroline when you came into the gallery . . . remember?'

Jenna's mind was rewinding. It was slowly coming back to her . . . there had been a telephone conversation when she was in St Ives. She remembered her father mentioning that he was delivering Gil's picture to the Covent Garden address.

A slow grin spread across her face. 'Well, you two kept this quiet.'

'There's more.' Daniel watched Jenna's face as he lifted Caroline's hand to display the diamond glinting on her finger. 'When something is right, there's just no point in waiting,' he said, gazing deep into Caroline's eyes.

Jenna's disbelieving stare went from one to the other, and then she rushed forward to hug them both.

Later, when Gil reached for Jenna's hand, he said, 'Of course, you know what this means?'

She nodded, eyes wide with excitement. 'It means that I can come back to Yorkshire with a clear conscience . . . that we can be married straight away!'

Gil's dark eyes were shining. 'How does next month suit you?' He laughed.

Her reply was lost as he swept her into his arms, but he didn't need the words. Her kiss told him all he wanted to know.

LUCY OF LARKHILL

Christina Green

Lucy is left to run her Dartmoor farm virtually on her own after a hired hand is injured. She does her best to carry on; though when she decides to sell her baked goods direct to the public, she is forced to admit that she is overwhelmed. She needs to hire a man to help on the farm, and her childhood friend Stephen might just be the answer. But as Lucy's feelings for him grow, she is more determined than ever to remain an independent spinster . . .

FINDING HER PERFECT FAMILY

Carol MacLean

Fleeing as far as she can from an unhappy home life, Amelia Knight arrives at the tropical island of Trinita to work as a nanny at the Grenville estate. As she battles insects and tropical heat, she must also fight her increasing attraction to baby Lucio's widowed father, Leo Grenville — a man whose heart has been broken, and thus is determined never to love again. Amelia must conquer stormy weather and reveal a desperate secret before she can find her perfect family to love forever.

THE SAPPHIRE

Fay Cunningham

Cass, a talented jeweller, wants a quiet life after having helped to solve a murder case. But life is anything but dull while she lives with her mother, an eccentric witch with a penchant for attracting trouble. Now Cass's father, who left the family when she was five, is back on the scene — as well handsome detective Noel Raven, with whom Cass has an electrifying relationship. As dangers both worldly and paranormal threaten Cass and those she loves, will they be strong enough to stand together and prevail?

TROUBLE IN PARADISE

Susan Udy

When Kat's mother, Ruth, tells her that her home and shop are under threat of demolition from wealthy developer Sylvester Jordan, Kat resolves to support her struggle to stay put. So when a mysterious vandal begins to target the shop, Sylvester — or someone in his employ — is their chief suspect. However, Sylvester is also offering Kat opportunities that will support her struggling catering business — and, worst of all, she finds that the attraction she felt to him in her school days is still very much alive . . .